The GENIUS *of the* GARDEN

To wake the soul by tender strokes of art,
To raise the genius, and to mend the heart.
Alexander Pope,

Prologue to Addison's 'Cato'

The GENIUS of the GARDEN

PETER VERNEY
MICHAEL DUNNE

Webb & Bower

MICHAEL JOSEPH

For Honor with love

First published in Great Britain 1989 by
Webb & Bower (Publishers) Limited
5 Cathedral Close, Exeter, Devon EX1 1EZ
in association with Michael Joseph Limited
27 Wright's Lane, London W8 5TZ

Penguin Books Ltd, Registered Offices: Harmondsworth, Middlesex,
England
Viking Penguin Inc, 40 West 23rd Street,
New York, NY 10010, USA
Penguin Books Australia Ltd, Ringwood, Victoria, Australia
Penguin Books Canada Ltd, 2801 John Street, Markham, Ontario,
Canada L3R 1D4
Penguin Books (NZ) Ltd, 182–190 Wairau Road, Auckland, New Zealand

Designed by Ron Pickless
Line drawings by Rosamund Gendle

Production by Nick Facer/Rob Kendrew

Text Copyright © 1989 Peter Verney/Michael Dunne
Photographs Copyright © 1989 Michael Dunne

British Library Cataloguing in Publication Data
Verney, Peter
    The genius of the garden.
    1. Gardens. Planning
    I. Title   II. Dunne, Michael
    712'.6

ISBN 0–86350–207–5

Typeset in Great Britain by J&L Composition Ltd, Filey, North Yorkshire

Colour reproduction by Peninsular Repro Service Ltd, Exeter, Devon

Printed and bound in Hong Kong

CONTENTS

FOREWORD

Why a garden? What is it in so many of us that craves a garden? Is it in a garden, and in gardening, that we find solace and tranquillity, an unburdening of the soul, and that age-old affinity with the soil which 'civilization' has done so much to obscure? The timeless elements of sun and shadow, stone, water and soil, foliage and flowers are all present and unchanging in gardens, but so they are in much of the countryside around us. So where is the magic, what is the genius, the spirit of creation, in our gardens?

The problems our gardening ancestors encountered as they created their Paradises were surprisingly similar to those we meet today, despite totally changed circumstances. In their solutions perhaps we may find some of our solutions; and by looking at their gardens with their eyes we may be able to see our own gardens with fresh eyes.

1 DISCIPLINE AND ORDER: OUR GARDENING HERITAGE

As our primitive ancestors pushed back the forests to protect their herds and open land for cultivation, human order began to impose itself on the natural world. In time that reordered world began to resemble a garden.

Persia is the commonly accepted birthplace of the garden as a deliberate concept. In the Persian garden geometric perfection and symbolism went hand in hand. Water, so necessary in wastes which would easily transform again to desert, was an essential ingredient.

Discipline and Order. A perfect blending of human discipline and natural order. This simple, uncluttered composition in a garden in Houston, Texas, creates an almost tangible sense of peace.

It represented the River of Life, and the four streams which created the cross or cruciform shape typical of the Persian garden were the four rivers of Paradise, where the true believer would eventually find peace. The cruciform theme, which was also essentially practical from the point of view of irrigation, was restful and easy on the eye. It has found expression throughout the long history of garden design and is as relevant now as ever.

Shut away from the harsh outside world, the Persian garden became a private oasis, a place to walk in comfort and in safety, shaded by trees, cooled by water and soothed by its cadences, a place adorned by pleasure pavilions – covered outdoor rooms – which were as much a part of the garden as path or rill, in all a place for 'secret and voluptuous enjoyments'.[1]

The Romans delighted in a happy blend of crisp order and verdant tranquillity. In their gardens which owed so much to the influence of the earlier Hellenistic world, porticos and promenades encouraged walk and conversation, while outdoor rooms invited alfresco meals. Space in many town houses was severely limited but most were built around a central open atrium or courtyard where water in the form of pool, fountain or rill, was an important element. Apart from the occasional citrus or grape, these were gardens to refresh the spirit rather than sustain the body. The Roman town garden was thus effectively an outdoor room, an urban oasis, part of a private, ordered world entered only by the privileged few.

And it is in the same light that we should view those surviving Islamic gardens in southern Spain. Here can be found the 'glorieta', the private paradise, or rather a succession of private paradises each complete in itself but creating a special sense of unity within a tight architectural frame. These are gardens of great significance in the evolution of garden design.

There were oases too in more temperate northern climes, but rather oases for the spirit rather than from the sun and the dust. When it was too dangerous to

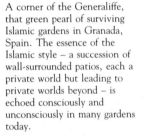

A corner of the Generaliffe, that green pearl of surviving Islamic gardens in Granada, Spain. The essence of the Islamic style – a succession of wall-surrounded patios, each a private world but leading to private worlds beyond – is echoed consciously and unconsciously in many gardens today.

where would be found arbours, *galleries* (the pergola of today), ornamental fountains and birds which sang as you strolled.

Thus was the late medieval garden, the 'goodlye gardeyn to walk ynne closed with high walls embattled'.[2] And there was tremendous charm in this garden through the intricacy of the picture and the transcendent love and pride of the gardener for her plot. For these 'feel' as though they were the special domain of the chatelaine and her ladies, indeed they were known as 'Lady's Gardens'. Such love transcends any deficiencies in design – ancestor perhaps, but in a more formalized way, of the delicious hodge-podge of the true cottage garden or the transparent delight of the specialist's garden where plant needs triumph over the designer's perennial cry of 'structure'.

Their medieval planter's palette was growing too with the introduction of more and more 'outlandish' flowers and spices brought back from the East by merchants and returning Crusaders. Introduced too

Left The Alhambra, Granada, Spain.

Below Essentially a modern version (in Philadelphia, Pennsylvania) of the concept of the medieval garden – crisp-edged, raised beds within a surrounding boundary and with a central feature to provide vertical accent.

venture beyond the castle walls what nicer way to relieve the monotony of medieval feudal life than to stroll in small enclosed gardens, referred to as the *hortus conclusus*, embellished with neat geometric knot beds.

Similar in concept were the monastic cloister gardens where strict division into individual beds was also observed. As the feudal and monastic lines developed so came the first signs of what the French later refined in the *jardin potager* – the comfortable blending of beauty, economy and utility in a decorative vegetable garden.

The few flowers then grown were principally for strewing on the floor or for nosegays and posies; the herbs, for medicinal, culinary and cosmetic uses. Native fruit trees and bushes were taken from the woods or brought by travellers and underwent improvement through culture and careful selection.

These gardens were formal and dignified. The cruciform shape was popular, often with a central fountain symbolizing the conjunction of God and Man. Generally the outside world was uninviting, and the contrast between order inside and the rude, cruel world beyond only confirmed how pleasant was their own private paradise. So the former simple cloister retreat became refined into the 'paradise garden', and then into the pleasaunce, a place for dalliance and knightly pleasures

were a number of design features derived from foreign, chiefly Islamic, influences, the most important of which was the wider and more imaginative use of water.

In the wake of comparative peace and prosperity in the fourteenth, fifteenth and sixteenth centuries in Europe – for gardens are a product of peace – garden design became less preoccupied with high enclosing walls. Significant elements for the future had appeared – crisp edges outlining a principally rectangular shape, conscious attention to scale and proportion, the use (and abuse) of stonework, fountainry and other garden ornament, particularly the supreme value of water and its manifold uses.

Hitherto the most visible signs of affluence and power had been the houses (and their contents) of the rich and famous. Now they were able to stretch out their properties, and sometimes their vanities, as affirmation of status and position.

It is in this light that we should regard the gardens of the great families of Renaissance Italy. As with their Roman antecedents – and salvaged Roman statuary reminded them of a golden past to which they sought to become the golden heirs – these gardens provided shade and space for walking and conversation. Many were built on hillsides so providing vista and prospect as well as the opportunity for spectacular use of water. And from the necessity of having purely functional links between levels their garden architects evolved a remarkable, and hitherto unique, unity of design by drawing together the firm horizontal of terrace and platform, so creating a whole new world of shadow. As counterpoint were the vertical elements which framed the view and provided the shade so necessary in this land of glaring sun. Here we see the first and most transcendent use of the Garden Trinity – evergreenery, stone, and water.

Visitors from the north were as astonished at these 'gardens one above another' as they were delighted by the spiritual excitement of the 'complete experience' of the Italian Renaissance garden.

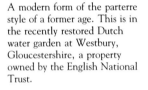

A modern form of the parterre style of a former age. This is in the recently restored Dutch water garden at Westbury, Gloucestershire, a property owned by the English National Trust.

There is something especially intimate about the Italian gardens of this period as their creators sought to bring back the classic feel of the Roman garden. In addition there is an air of mystery and secrecy in the wooded siderooms, the *boschetti*, where symbolism and allegory found expression in sculpture, stonework or fountain. The boundary too was still distinct so keeping the whole apart from the countryside around, a point of great evolutionary significance.

However, here we see the germs of the subtle compromise we seek to find between the soft touch of Nature and the heavy hand of Man, between pattern and 'wild varietie'.

So, by way of the Italian garden architects of the fifteenth century, the meek and modest knot garden of monastery and manor house, after developing into the more elaborate parterre, ultimately became the grandiloquent formal garden of France. None more splendid than those created from 1660 for Louis the Magnificent, the Sun King himself, at the hands of the master, André Le Nôtre.

These and similar compositions, stretching as far as the eye could see, were more than exercises in symmetry and balance. They absorbed the broader horizons of northern France, dominating the generally flat terrain as the Sun King dominated his France of the day. The uncompromising hand of 'formalism', descended on the countryside as the etiquette and rigidity of the salon moved out of doors. Here indeed was a stage setting worthy of the most magnificent court in Europe.

The spectator was principally required to marvel at the greatness of the creation and above all at the greatness of the monarch who could command such magnificence and extravagance, which was partly the purpose.

But there was little inducement to walk to the end of the endless avenues. The gently trickling rivulet which had so beguiled the Persian in his Paradise, had become the drenching spray of massive *jets d'eau*, while reflection on acres of open water brought Heaven to earth, a symbolism to satisfy even what his many enemies called the insatiable ambitions of Louis XIV. The reticence of the medieval gardens which had been such a solace and pleasure to those who dallied there, had become a travesty, chilling in its remoteness and over-bearing in its mastery of Nature. Sheer size

Above Vaux-le-Vicomte.

dwarfed mere mortals, not so much before God, but before this particular god on earth.

On closer examination, however, the pronounced axial theme created an exciting unity to the whole composition and gave a strong sense of discipline and order. Architecture itself and the 'architecture' of extreme formalism dominated the stage so that the garden became in effect an extension of the house. 'Crossway' fountains and statuary were integrated so as to provide perspective and rhythm. Symmetry and balance were maintained on the principal axes but a degree of variety and surprise was achieved through the use of design tricks and subtle elaborations which, though in no way detracting from the strength of the overall design yet created an unfolding succession of visual events – indeed Louis was so anxious his guests appreciate these that he produced his own guidebook. While in the wings behind crisply trimmed hedges, which themselves contributed varied texture, were many intimate bosquets each with its special delight or wonder. The whole had to be seen against the back-cloth of dark uncompromising woodland, while the scale of the foreground had to be massive to contend with the massive scale of everything else. Here the water, which rushed to the surface after any excavation in this land of high water table and which in the past had been so imaginatively used for defensive purposes, became noble canals and *miroirs d'eau* at the hands of the master.

The broad concept of uncompromising expanses of terrace and parterre so effective in northern France, and which looked remarkably similar come summer come winter, was slavishly copied, with varying success, in many countries of Europe. It was not, however, successful in Holland where the land was generally divided into small plots owned by middle-class burghers, who, curtailed by parallel irrigation ditches, conceived a throwback to the medieval *hortus conclusus*. So they developed a style depending largely on geometric flower beds, toy waterways and elaborate decoration all within a firm

The traditional Discipline and Order seen in the archetype English eighteenth-century mansion (in Wiltshire). The dignity and restraint of the architecture call for a similar dignity and restraint in the more intimate design of the garden.

enclosure – a world of painted tree trunks, bushes fashioned into discs, plumes and fans, and gardens which were described by travellers as made for dwarfs. Thus the considerable gardening skills of the Dutch found expression in exquisite topiary and meticulous, inch-perfect flower beds, fitting homes for the spring bulbs of which they were particularly fond, especially the tulip.

Nor was it suited to England. Here was a mixture of landscape unrivalled outside her shores and a climate more gentle than that enjoyed in much of France. Further, the feeling of inevitability, discipline and logic of the Le Nôtre school was as unsuited to the English temperament as it was to the English landscape. The glories of the style were briefly aped around some larger

mansions but to many this was an alien infliction for the French gardens were primarily to be looked at from afar, and, preferably from above, rather than to walk in and to live in. For where in the acres of stone, the miles of formal avenues, the lavish fountains and waterworks was there place for the soft contours of the English countryside? How could the traditional, sympathetic use of land, the lush grass and superb individual trees be incorporated in such a composition? These were surely far more eloquent of the national temperament than the grandeur that was Le Nôtre, even in English clothes?

For in the rigidity of these great formal gardens of the age there was little sense of discovery, no room for hills or hollows, or winding paths. The whole was on such a scale that plants – and their plant range was still limited for this was before the days of the great plant collectors – looked insignificant and the creation more like a massive theatre than a garden; a picture perfected, inanimate and soulless. There was surprise, of a sort, in wondering what lay through the gaps in the flanking walls of greenery. But if they had been able to read what was written one hundred years later by the foremost landscape gardener of his day, Humphry Repton (1725–1818): 'The eye, or rather the mind, is never long delighted with that which it surveys without effort, at a single glance, and therefore sees without exciting curiosity or interest'[3] – many would have agreed wholeheartedly. It was as though in England the borrowed 'formality' of the Le Nôtre school was an aberration, an alien theme torn from its true context. We can see now that the pendulum of gardening taste which has characterized garden design through the ages and successively oscillated between the formal, geometric, and the informal, more natural, styles of gardening, had swung too far.

There was growing acknowledgement that though the parterre was useful and intriguing and drew attention to the ground-plan as well as complementing the verticality of a house, the style could never do justice to plants. There is a pronounced feeling about this period that something was lacking, also that no one quite knew what. On consideration, it began to crystallize that this was the serenity only to be attained by true harmony between Man and his natural surroundings.

Foremost among the opponents in England of rigid formality in garden design were the essayist, poet and statesman Joseph Addison (1672–1719) who used the periodical *The Spectator* as his platform, and the poet Alexander Pope (1688–1744) who aired his views in the columns of *The Guardian*. They had a great deal of fun. Topiary, a Dutch predilection, came in for scathing criticism as 'tonsured greenery', but their real target was formality in garden design in general. As Addison wrote: 'Our British gardeners instead of humouring Nature, love to deviate from it as much as possible. Our trees arise in Cones, Globes and Pyramids. We see the mark of the scissars upon every Plant and Bush.'[4] 'Nor is any Thing more shocking,' wrote one of their supporters, 'than a stiff, regular garden. Where after we have seen one quarter thereof, the very same is repeated in all the remaining Parts, so we are tired, instead of being further entertained with something new as expected.'[5]

And so at the hands of such creative minds as Stephen Switzer (1682–1745), Charles Bridgeman (d 1738), William Kent (?1685–1748) and Lancelot 'Capability' Brown (1716–1783) the formal garden as exemplified by the French and Dutch schools gave way to the freer conceptions of the Landscape School. Many gardens of great, albeit formal charm were turned into 'pompous solitudes' of unrelieved parkland of sweeping vistas with clumps and belts of trees. In this, a marriage of contour and planting, the garden was deprived of first its bounds and then its flowers which were banished to distant walled kitchen gardens.

Soon enough reaction set in, for this 'natural' style of gardening was anything but natural. The house was left 'gazing by itself in the middle of a park'[6] Horace Walpole, Earl of Orford (1717–1797), politician and keen gardener remarked. Rallying to the cause, a new breed of satyrical writers sharpened their wits and their pens inveighing against shaven lawns 'in one undulating sweep and scattered clumps, that nod at one another. Each stiffly waving to its formal brother'.[7] But in the right place the landscaped park could be majestically successful:

Who drew o'er the surface, did you or did I,
The smooth-flowing outline, that steals from the eye,
The soft undulations, both distant and near,
That heave from the ground, and yet scarcely appear?

Who thinn'd, and who group'd and who scatter'd the
trees?
Who bade the slopes fall with such elegant ease?
Who cast them in shade, and who plac'd them in
light?
Who bade them divide, and who bade them unite?[8]

Capability Brown, the 'incomparable magician', died
in 1783 and moving, seemingly without effort, into his
shoes after a brief interval came Humphry Repton, the
first to describe himself as a landscape gardener.
Flowers were now brought back to the vicinity of the
house, while terraces were once more in vogue.
Though many of Repton's landscape schemes were
majestic they were generally less sweeping than those of
the earlier landscape period. In these one can see a
formidable transitional talent at work, ameliorating the
worst excesses of what the critics condemned as the
'Bare and the Bald'. A number of people were beginning to mourn the passing of many a fine garden,
Repton among them, and he sadly wrote: 'No trace
now remains of [Italian style] balustraded terraces of
masonry, magnificent flights of steps, arcades and
architectural grottoes, lofty clipped hedges, with niches
and recesses enriched by sculpture.'[9]

However, there was one especially important theme
in the approach to garden design which had begun to
creep in, although it did not reach its full flowering
until one hundred or more years later.

At first gardens had been inward looking, eschewing
anything to do with the native hostility of the outside
world. Then Nature became a true partner as gardens
and gardeners started to look outwards beyond the
formality of the area nearest the house, be it from
terrace, loggia or outdoor room. In a highly significant
statement Alexander Pope declared: 'He gains all
points who pleasingly confounds, surprises, varies and
conceals the bounds'.[10] This infers a more pronounced
'stroll' aspect in garden design than hitherto, an
influence far nearer the Italian Renaissance paradise
than the instant glance style of the formal French
school. They were in fact beginning to experience and
enjoy the delights of sequence, although the product
was not all Italian for after all the Italians, as one
jaundiced traveller put it, 'understand the excellencies
of art; but they have no idea of the beauties of
nature'.[11]

Thus the groundwork was laid for the appreciation of
Chinese, and later the Japanese, approach to gardening
where each constituent becomes integral to a marvel-
lously harmonious composition. In short, the concept
of multitudinous aspects when paths were less a means
of access to one or other part of the garden than a
succession of points from which to enjoy from many
angles an unfolding series of delights. This is a
cornerstone of garden design and it affords manifold
scope for the artifices of the garden creator.

A principal influence behind the breaking of the
landscape mould was William Chambers (1726–96)
who as a young man had gone to China as servant of
the Swedish East India Company. He set himself up as
an architect in London, and an influential introduction
secured a commission to design a number of ornamental buildings at Kew Gardens, including the cele-
brated Pagoda. Then in 1772 he bounced on a highly
impressionable world his own impressions of Chinese
gardens and architecture in A Dissertation on Oriental
Gardening.

The essence of the new style was change – change of
focus, changes of scene, and infinite variety in a
succession of garden pictures. Clever devices were
employed to make the wanderer pause and linger – a
different paving texture, a bend in a path, a seat
inviting rest and giving on to some little piece of sheer
gardening delight. These were gardens of illusion where
features such as bridges, rocks, even individual trees
suggested images. Overall they provided the complete
experience of the Italian Renaissance garden in new,
quite different and supposedly Oriental clothing.

It is recognized now that Chambers' Dissertation was
really a gigantic hoax and that he used the unwitting
'Chinese' as a platform to attack the Landscape School
and put across his own singular and imaginative views
on garden and landscape design. It had been nearly
forty years before and as a boy of sixteen that he had
made his sole trip to China, and in the second edition
of the Dissertation he acknowledged his joke.

Hoax or not, Chambers' conceptions were remarkably prescient of how garden design would develop.
This was long before the explosion of plant types and
plant species which is normally reckoned to have
provided the essential stimulus behind those changes in
garden design which were to take place one hundred
years later. It seems that Sir William Chambers may

truly be considered the prophet of modern garden design.

The more 'natural' school of gardening of the later decades of the eighteenth century is one to which we easily relate today. Here is something we can recognize as a garden, a reincarnation of the Persian Paradise, or the oasis of Islam but without walls and which treats the countryside with sympathy. A place where one could walk with pleasure and enjoy an ordered informality and which gave true scope to 'the Poet's feeling and the Painter's eye'[12] of the garden creator.

Chambers had sown the seed. Debate had prospered. More significantly the fundamentals of garden design were at last being thought through. The pendulum of garden taste, which had so extravagantly swung towards the formal in the seventeenth century and the less formal in the decades that followed, was beginning to steady. Perhaps Chambers, architect of the theme which was to have such a devastating impact on the European garden – for soon what was called the *jardin anglo-chinois* came to be widely adopted – should be allowed the last word: 'It is I think obvious that neither the artful nor the simple style of Gardening . . . is right: the one being too extravagant a deviation from nature; . . . the other insipid and vulgar: a judicious mixture of both would certainly be more perfect than either.'[13]

Superficially, therefore, the swing of the pendulum

Many ethnic garden designs transported to an alien setting simply do not work; although they may capture the form, they fail to capture the spirit. However, this Japanese-style garden in Locust Valley, New York, admirably achieves this difficult translation.

to a more 'formalized' type of garden in the Victorian era would seem strange. Until, that is, one appreciates that the informality of previous 'natural' garden styles is built on a concept of discipline and order as profound as any conceived by Le Nôtre or his followers. For informality without structure is nothing but a mess.

Gardens are an expression of the society of the time. The great Renaissance gardens of Italy were as much statements of their owner's confidence as they were superb creations in their own right. Versailles was, as much as anything, an attempt to make Nature curtsy to an earthly and supremely confident being. So too in Victorian gardens confidence shines like the sun – confidence in their society, confidence in industrial wealth and above all confidence in themselves. Here was Man's dominance over Nature in as profound a way, although on a different scale, as any in gardening history. It expressed itself in tremendous experimentation, in startling ingenuity and in an eclecticism in garden design which has never been surpassed. This took on many guises – 'Greek' gardens, 'Roman' gardens, 'Egyptian' and many other supposedly foreign derivations found favour. Most were shallow copies and wholly unsuited to their setting – it is difficult, for instance, to find much authenticity in an 'Egyptian' garden in an English drizzle! With the opening of Japan to the West 'Japanese' gardens also became popular. However, the difficulties of translating the form of a garden without its true and essential spirit can never have been more thoroughly demonstrated than when a Japanese guest being shown round his garden by a proud host was heard to remark, 'It is indeed wonderful, I have never seen anything like it in my life.'[14]

In gardening terms it was a time when the old and new cross-fertilizations came to exciting fruition in the mixing pan of time, usage and taste. Superimposed was the explosion of new plant material coming from abroad, much of it from different climates. Prior to 1840 the 'exotics', as they were termed – and some proved far hardier than anyone imagined – were the province of the very rich for only they could afford the luxury of glass, but the manufacture of cheap glass and the wide use of iron supports for glasshouses revolutionized the garden. Simultaneously the use of the cylinder lawn mower (invented in 1830) opened a whole new world of horticultural practice. How better to display these new treasures which everyone was raising than in vista or island beds in a sea of closely cropped grass to both set off their beauty and express the order and discipline that ruled their own lives?

Ordered lines of massed bedding in a grassy frame, the up-dated version of the old medieval knot garden and French parterre and a living pattern, were satisfying up to a point. It was possible to look at specimen trees – such as the amazing Monkey-Puzzle or Chile Pine (*Araucaria*) – stuck in a lawn, for few of the burgeoning middle-class gardeners, who now made up the mass of gardening enthusiasts, had space for such extravagances as arboreta. But what of the other new and exciting trees and shrubs which were beginning to flood the country and which in shape, texture, colour and form offered more than the limited flowering season of the semi-tender exotics? How could they be best added to the gardener's palette? And so the geometric 'formality' of the Victorian garden began to crumble. There was an underlying realization that the garden offered more than essentially single-plane, (two dimensional), pictures and that what the bedding enthusiasts had been attempting was to superimpose an alien design. Like Le Nôtre and others they had tried to dominate Nature and by doing so had denied themselves true gardening fulfilment.

This too was in tune with the growing awareness that Man and Nature must live in harmony and people were being urged to look on their natural heritage with new eyes. This was the age of Emerson and Thoreau, and of the Pre-Raphaelites and their imitators, with Ruskin at the height of his influence. It was also the cue for the arrival on the gardening scene of two of the most dominating figures in garden history, on both sides of the Atlantic, in the last hundred years – William Robinson (1838–1935) and later his disciple, Gertrude Jeykll (1843–1932). In terms of garden design, the former is noted for his handling of perennial plants in the garden, and looking at the garden with 'new eyes'; the latter for developing those concepts and her own incomparable 'artist's eye' for colour interpretations. Both would surely have subscribed to Shakespeare's lines:

This is an Art
Which does mend Nature: change it rather: but
The art itself is Nature[15]

Thus by the 1920s the pattern of modern gardening was beginning to emerge – and it is a pattern that has remained largely undisturbed since. This is the blend between the 'formal' and the 'informal' – but the latter underpinned by sound structure. The pendulum has come to rest.

What remains is to adopt and adapt, incorporate and put into garden form the shape and aspirations of horticultural and social and economic change which has progressively led to fewer and fewer observing rather than participating gardeners.

Have we found a balance between the 'formal' and the 'informal', and with it the underlying need for order and discipline? More important, the understanding that though each historic gardening style can be translated into the modern garden there is such a medley of periods and influences at play here that the whole, if we are not careful, will become a confusion?

Changing notions of leisure have altered our approach to gardening and economics have made our gardens generally smaller. But within the frame we have now created we can absorb horticultural developments, plant improvements and the products of plant breeding, new botanical discoveries and enhancing cultural methods. What we seek now is plant luxuriance within an architectural framework; a garden in balance with its surroundings and with the home for which it provides a fitting setting; ease of cultivation and ease of maintenance; maximum effect for minimum effort; an all-year paradise as satisfying in winter as it is in spring, summer or autumn and the extension of the house into the garden, the garden into the house.

But in general our aspirations have not altered much in 400 years. As one Abraham Cowley said in the 1650s: 'I never had any other desire so strong, and so like to covetousness, as that one which I have had always, that I might be master at last of a small house and large garden, with very moderate conveniences joined to them, and there dedicate the remainder of my life only to the culture of them and study of nature.'[16]

2 PATHWAY TO PARADISE

My garden sweet, enclosed with walles strong
Embanked with benches to sytt and take my rest,
The Knots so enkotted it cannot be espres't,
With arbors and alyes so pleasant and so dulce. [1]

Visiting gardens has become a principal leisure activity today, but how many of us try to analyse what we sense when first we see a garden? We may not all agree with the sixteenth-century poet Hawkins who said that a garden is a 'Monopolie of all Pleasure and Delights that are on Earth amassed together' [2].

There would seem to be two broad approaches to garden appreciation, indeed to design appreciation generally. The first is the Islamic approach – one is faced with a bland door in a blank wall giving nothing away and promising as little, but open that door . . . and paradise is revealed. This is what one might call the 'wow!' emotion of instant impact. Then there is the Western approach, more gradual and more subtle – the appetite is titillated, the curiosity aroused. . .and paradise slowly unfolds. This is the 'woo' approach. If we can find a perfect blending of the two we are surely a long way on the path to the paradise we seek ourselves.

The essence of the 'wow' approach to garden design is, naturally, that the 'wow' feature should remain unsuspected for as long as possible. When first seen it must stop us in our tracks, so bewitch us that we are temporarily breathless. This heart-stopper may be a magnificent view, an inspired blend of colour or texture, a plant excelling in sight or scent – for by no means need this be a visual experience alone – or the creation of a little piece of paradise which by planning or design or even, and quite often, through pure chance, utterly transports the imagination by its charm.

In some respects the subtlety of the 'woo' approach is harder to achieve but by careful planning and planting the viewer's step can be anticipated, even dictated. We are gently lured by the half-hidden, the heard-but-not-seen or the tantalizing scent from an unseen source. We glimpse features through window or open door, through a half-screening trellis, hedge or fence. Perhaps our curiosity is aroused by the seduction of a path curving into mystery, or from stone pillars or columnar trees standing sentinel before a gap or gate which invites exploration, even from the distant murmur of water.

The Reverend William Mason in his poem *The English Garden* (1772) understood the art of the seductive approach:

Admit it partially, and half exclude
And half reveal its graces in this path,
How long so'er the wanderer roves, each step
Shall wake fresh beauties; each short point provide
A different picture, new, and yet the same. [3]

The Grand Tour in Europe in the seventeenth and eighteenth centuries almost always included visits to the great Renaissance gardens of Italy. From the accounts of those pilgrims it is clear they were hugely impressed, even moved by what they saw. As a later traveller wrote, the Italian Renaissance garden was a place of 'striking contrast; of sudden and thrilling surprise; of close confinement as a prelude to boundless freedom; of scorching sun as a prelude to welcome shade or cooling river; of monotony, even of ugliness, set for a foil to enchanting beauty. . .' [4] These were gardens which engaged all the senses, the mind and soul as well, in truth a 'complete experience'.

'WOW!' Beyond this mundane, workaday entrance to a garden in County Tipperary, Ireland, lies a special piece of paradise, yet there is little inkling of this from outside.

In contrast, at first glance there was little surprise or sense of discovery in the great stage sets of the formal French school, at least to the untutored majority of observers, for many of Le Nôtre's subtleties in controlling level, vista and contour remained unrecognized. On the other hand, obvious surprise was of considerable importance in the designs of more natural schools of gardening. Surprise is a unique experience, as the critics did not hesitate to point out, but after surprise comes the more durable pleasure of anticipation. 'One never tires of . . .' is a remark often heard, particularly of views and vistas. The viewer knows what comes next – he has seen it a dozen times – yet this in no way diminishes the pleasure of seeing it again and again.

It is with this mingling of the sensations of surprise, or rather discovery, and anticipation that we view gardens, or any work of art for that matter. Our gardening efforts are designed essentially to satisfy the senses, to help create that 'complete experience' that so moved the eighteenth century visitors to Italian gardens. But sometimes one is left wondering just what certain modern gardens are trying to achieve and if their owners really find true satisfaction.

Much of that satisfaction hinges on discipline and order. Within each of us lurks the inherent recognition of accord, of symmetery, of the rightness of things. This is as true of the garden as of any work of Man. A picture, a building, a piece of sculpture either jars on our sensibilities or it looks right. It looks right in itself; it looks right in its relationship with the features around; it gives a feeling of resting easy in its context, and then in our hearts we rejoice and in our souls we feel content at the discovery of peace in a balanced composition.

This notion of geometric harmony was basic to the concepts of the fifteenth-century Italian architect Alberti and it found glorious expression in the early Italian Renaissance garden. Above all the Renaissance mind sought Order and Reason, and it found realization in strict symmetry and proportion, even in the garden which was seen as continuing the sequence of indoor rooms. In practical terms, Alberti and his followers manipulated space to provide a unity of design closely related to the harmony and proportions of the accompanying architecture. By means of a process of tranquil progression, house and garden were merged so that the formality of the house and its

immediate surrounds gradually gave way to the less formal areas of what Alberti himself called the 'delicacy of gardens'. The result was both restful and satisfying.

Alberti's concepts are as valid today as they ever were. However, even Alberti admitted that it is often easier to see where a design 'is ill-done than it is to lay down rules for the doing of it', adding ' . . . the very smallest parts of the work, if they are set in their right places, add to the beauty of the whole; if they are placed in mean or improper situations, though excellent in themselves, they become mean . . . so that nothing can be added or taken away, decreased or enlarged, or differently placed without detracting from the grace and beauty of the whole.'[5]

This clear conception of what is intended to be the ultimate design is crucial to the garden creator: 'Every wall, path, stone and flower bed has its . . . relative value to the central idea. Garden schemes should have a backbone, a central idea, beautifully phrased',[6] was how Sir Edwin Lutyens, Gertrude Jekyll's partner in the creation of many a fine garden, put it. In many gardens this phrasing, the central idea, or the progression of ideas, is obscure or obscured by too much detail. There is a tendency to over-elaborate, especially in small gardens. The wood disappears and one sees only the trees; or, put another way, the garden is lost among the flowers.

There needs to be a clear connection between the various elements, when that is missing the whole jars on the sensibilities. The eye must be led effortlessly from one plane to another, from one level to another, from one area to another. Most important of all is the balance between the horizontal and the vertical.

To build, to plant, whatever you intend,
To rear the column, and the arch to bend,
To swell the terras, or to sink the grot;
In all let Nature never be forgot.
Still follow Sense, of every art the Soul.
Parts answ'ring parts, shall slide into a whole.[7]

The Oriental garden achieved this essential unity by a process of gentle assimilation. Oriental garden-makers sought and found complete harmony with Nature and by strict observance of scale and even stricter adherence to the balance of the composition created magical gardens of mood and imagery.

In studying unity in composition there is a distinct parallel with the problems met by the landscape painter. As one of the greatest, John Constable, wrote: 'Every piece of ground is distinguished by certain properties; it is either tame or bold; gentle or rude; continued or broken; if any variety, inconsistent with these properties, be intruded, it has no other effect than to weaken one idea, without raising another.'[8]

This unity can be achieved in many ways – by using similar material for house, path or other stonework, through linkage, by gradual progression of colour and tone. For instance, bright colour or heavy tone receding into blues, greens or greys gives not only a sense of distance but also one of a continuous progression which the eye finds satisfying.

A garden which can be seen at a glance, with everything in the shop window, lacks interest, excitement and the anticipation of discovery. Even on the smallest plot the attention can be caught and redirected by some detail – a seat, a piece of statuary, some garden ornament, an architectural plant, a sudden splash of colour, a bend in a path – and all can draw the eye even if the space is too small to draw the step. This half-hidden promise of excitement giving a hint of something out of the ordinary lends vitality to the scene without disturbing its essential harmony.

Constable averred that 'some drama of light and shade must underlie all compositions'.[9] This is as true of garden design as of great landscape painting. For light is never still. A lawn can sparkle and scintillate with the morning dew, and in minutes appear drab as the dew dries. Water can reflect scurrying clouds then as dusk falls become a mirror of steely grey. And never does a garden appear more magical than in the strong slanting and changing light of early morning or late afternoon.

> Yet shall the graceful line forget to please,
> If border'd close by sidelong parallels,
> Nor duly mixt with those opposing curves
> That give the charm of contrast.[10]

Left A perfect 'formal' woodland scene in azalea time in Houston, Texas, and a typical 'stroll' garden. Here in western guise is the essence of what our garden ancestors recognized as the Oriental influence – a sequence of gradually unfolding delights, each enchanting in itself but also part of an harmonious whole. By clever planning and planting it is possible to make the walker pause wherever the designer wishes. The presence and siting of the stone obelisk is an additional touch of genius emphasizing rather than detracting from the flowing lines of the background planting.

Opposite Manipulation of texture, both growing and artificial, is one of the most potent weapons in the garden creator's armoury. This paving in the Alhambra, Granada, Spain, leads the eye onwards by its soothing repeating pattern, but the subtleties within the general design banish tedium. There is an atmosphere here of cool content which is heightened by the general greenness in the planting. The overall effect, however, would be enhanced were the low hedges trimmed at the bottom as well as at the top. This would produce an additional horizontal line of considerable significance.

It is contrast which keeps the eye active, and it comes in many forms – comparison of height, of form and shape, of tone and texture, between the straight and the sinuous, between shade and sun, between the formal and the informal.

To some extent we have concentrated on the visual sense in the creation of our paradise, yet as Erasmus put it, the garden is 'designed for the entertainment of the Sight and Smell and the refreshment of the Very Mind'.[11] It was this unification of the senses, the 'complete experience' of the Italian gardens of the Renaissance which so captivated seventeenth- and eighteenth- century visitors. For in a garden what we actually seek is a succession of sensuous intervals, part emotion, part reality, whose ...

> Greatest art is aptly to conceal;
> To lead, with secret guile, the prying sight
> To where component parts may best unite,
> And form one beauteous, nicely blended whole,
> To charm the eye and capitivate the soul.[12]

In creating a garden we are dealing with a unique medium, one that is growing and changing. Worse, whereas with a single stroke of his brush an artist can rub out his efforts and start again, anyone wishing to create a garden must wait for at least one and possibly

'Straight lines are the best foil to the grace of natural curves in plant and flowers.' (Ruskin.) Here the crisp raised edging to these borders provide a perfect foil to the luxuriant planting.

Opposite At first glance the white vase full of gaudy annuals perched on its red stone plinth is too sharp a contrast to the restraint of the rest of planting and background. But the more one studies the picture the more it becomes apparent that this unusual and original solution cleverly complements the sharp peak of the barn against the sky, throws the emphasis of the composition to one side and acts as a skilful foil to the irregular pavings.

A little touch of Irish magic in a garden in County Tipperary. Although it is almost impossible to tell, the tree in the gap is the better part of twenty feet behind the line of the hedge. It provides the perfect balance to a beautifully balanced view.

two growing seasons before he or she makes the uncomfortable discovery that the wrong plant is in the right place, or the right plant is in the wrong place, or the wrong plant is in the wrong place.

Thus gardening is a process of continuing experimentation. No wonder it is sometimes said that a garden is a place where plants are continually on the move! In pursuing an idea of perfection yet hoping, in their hearts, never quite to achieve it, true gardeners display great perversity. But their reasons are not hard to understand, for 'whereas every other pleasure commonly fills some of our sences, and that only with delight, this [gardening] makes all our sences swimme in pleasure, and that with infinite varietie . . .'[13] Indeed in the eleventh century St Anselm declared it dangerous to sit in a garden near roses for they satisfied both sight and smell, and were likely to encourage the singing of songs and the telling of stories, which satisfied the ears. In his opinion worldly temptations were harmful in proportion to the number of senses they delighted.

To lead with secret guile, the prying sight
To where component parts may best unite,
And form one beauteous, nicely blended whole,
To charm the eye and captivate the soul. (Richard Payne Knight.)

And it is possible to achieve this in even the smallest garden, as here in Rye, Sussex.

27

3 Transitions and Links

The stately mansion rising to the view,
But mix'd and blended, ever let it be
A mere component part of what you see.
For if in solitary pride it stand,
'tis but a lump, encumbering the land,
A load of inert matter, cold and dead,
Th' excrescence of the lawn that round it spread. [1]

Arguments against the Landscape School and its preoccupation with park at the expense of garden flamed for much of the latter half of the eighteenth century, and from time to time flare even now, although practical economics makes them somewhat academic. Foremost among the opponents of the 'Bare and the Bald' were two neighbouring Herefordshire landowners, Sir Uvedale Price (1747–1829) and Richard Payne Knight (1750–1824). The former, much to his later regret had succumbed to the prevailing fashion

The 'platform' surrounding this house in the Cotswolds, Gloucestershire, is quite evident. The differing textures of the lawn and the field, and the division between the two created by the low wall which edges a stream, provide the balance to a perfectly balanced composition. The eye instinctively compares the height of the house with the distance to the wall, and finds it satisfying and harmonious.

and in 1794 we find him writing wistfully: '. . . I remember that even this garden (so infinitely inferior to those of Italy) had an air of decoration . . . a distinction from mere unembellished nature, which, whatever the advocates for extreme simplicity may allege, is surely essential to an ornamental garden . . .'[2]

The problem was succinctly put by the greatest advocate of the formal school of garden design in Victorian England, Sir Reginald Blomfield. In 1889 he wrote: 'The question briefly stated is this: Are we, in laying out our gardens to ignore the house, and to reproduce uncultivated Nature to the best of our ability in the garden? Or are we to treat house and garden as inseparable factors in one homogenous whole, which are to co-operate for one premeditated result?'[3] One who was quite certain of the answer was Sir George Sitwell, author of *An Essay On The Making of Gardens* published in 1909. He strongly disapproved of houses 'apparently dropped from the skies', adding that 'a house requires a platform as a statue requires a pedestal'.[4]

The success or failure of a garden design often hangs on the handling of the PLATFORM on which the house rests and which can so effectively 'anchor' the scene – and by platform we usually mean terraces or patios (paved areas) or decks (wooden-floored extensions of the house). Here is the jumping-off point, the transitional zone where the building meets the softer, less clearly delineated living world. This is an area which should unite house and garden either by projecting the character of the house, or by borrowing that of the garden and directing it inwards.

However, a platform can be created in other ways, indeed on smaller plots the entire garden is the platform. The crucial point is that there should be a clear change of texture between the transitional area nearest the house and that of the rest of the garden or landscape.

Le Nôtre maintained that a terrace should be of a width equivalent to the height to the eves. This is a fair guideline but clearly much depends on the site. What

Here in another Cotswold garden the steps and distant wall with its peculiar recess provide the edge of the 'platform'.

'The garden must not be considered as a thing in itself, but as a gallery of foregrounds designed to set off the soft hues of the distance.' (Sir George Sitwell.)

In many settings the colour in the foreground might distract from the view. But here the backcloth provided by the mountains of Provence in this garden in Tignet, near Grasse, France, is so powerful that a more restrained planting would be altogether too muted.

is important is that the platform should not be too narrow, for the eye can more easily accommodate an excess of width than a dimension which is too mean. Further, a broader platform will give the impression of reducing the height of a tall house. Judicious planning and planting on and around the platform can also lead the eye away from a building's more hideous aspects.

It is this balance brought about through the correct shape, feature and proportion of the platform that can be so restful on the eye, and consequently on the spirit. But how often is this the case? Some houses appear to be strangers in their gardens, prisoners in a foreign landscape, incongruous and uneasy in their setting as though they and their designers had conspired to ensure that they dominated their natural surroundings by brash, uncompromising assertion. Sir George Sitwell again: 'The house is at war with the landscape and the landscape with the house, each has a different tale to tell and no natural beauty of flower or tree can relieve us from the shock of contradiction and the pain of incongruity.'[5]

So, ideally, the house should sit comfortably on its platform. Be in proportion to its setting, in harmony in both material and style. Be in sympathy with its surroundings. In short, it should look right. And its rightness will be sensed immediately by someone stepping from the house into the garden.

The importance of this first impression should never be underestimated for it sets the scene for the enjoyment of the garden, or the reverse. Even before that exciting moment when the ceiling becomes the sky, expectations can be raised by glimpses of the garden through window or doorway. And as soon as one actually crosses the threshold it is possible to sense whether the whole is a balanced composition or not. This often is more a subconscious than conscious act for one is virtually still indoors, yet by design, by planting layout, through unified texture or composition, by a dozen different devices the eye is being drawn towards the less formal area of the garden.

Thus the platform becomes an extension of the house: platform and house, in effect, become partners. They sit well together, easy in proportion and in balance. Yet platform and house can also dominate a garden as uncomfortably as the house alone unless there is a strong unifying influence. These all important HORIZONTAL LINKS can be created by paths, drives,

avenues or tree-lined walks, pergolas, walls, fences or hedges, by stretches of lawn, paving, gravel or water, by slopes and flights of steps . . . in fact by any medium or structure which provides a longitudinal dimension or area of continuous texture. Horizontal links can also be created by planting, by water, or by the subtle use of focal points.

PATHS are the means most of us choose to link the house/platform with the garden, and one part of the garden with another. Indeed in many gardens the paths are the main element of design and pattern. They are a convenient way of dividing up a plot and giving it form. But all paths – radiating, intersecting, broad or narrow, long or short – should lead somewhere. There is something fundamentally unsatisfactory about cul-de-sacs.

A garden requires a firm, positive underlying structure and it is perfectly possible to base much of that skeleton on paths, although there is the risk that too many paths cutting up an area will spoil the garden. But paths can contribute much more than mere 'bones' to a garden,

Opposite A brilliant piece of garden design in Houston, Texas. Linkage here is by paths, hedges and planting. But the real touch of genius is the manner in which the eye is led (and the foot would inevitably follow) towards the distant piece of sculpture framed by the gap in the hedge and the rounded sentinel topiary. A particularly clever feature is the sharp bend in the right-hand bed of white azaleas. Although seen here on a large scale, there is no reason why such optical cheats cannot be reproduced on a smaller one.

Below A 'roosting place', as garden seats were once called, where the view outwards is as important as that inwards.

for by clever planning it is possible not only to lead the eye and the step, but also dictate the viewer's pace and direction of interest. If that process can be made so subtle that it becomes almost subliminal, then a gardening paradise is surely within our grasp.

Paths can also add immeasurably to the mystery of a garden. A path curling round a corner makes us curious about what lies beyond. A change of texture or pattern in a path sets us wondering. An ornament placed at an intersection or crossway draws us like a magnet.

Path width is important. Ideally a path should be wide enough for two people to walk along side by side. Wide paths give a sense of ease and relaxation. They are made for sauntering and belong to a world where time means little. Indeed it is uncommonly difficult to hurry along a broad path. However, the width should be proportionate to its length and proportionate too to the height of any wall, hedge or background running parallel with it. A narrower path can be fussy and insubstantial, unless it winds mysteriously and invitingly into the depth of trees or shrubbery.

WALLS also make satisfactory horizontal links, and provide a vertical element too. Walls of stone, brick or concrete, or hedges which are natural growing walls, are connecting as well as dividing elements. HEDGES of course require maintenance and in their young days a lot of tending and feeding. They can also dry out and impoverish the nearby soil. There are a limited number of plants which will grow through hedges, and planting too near a hedge is almost always a mistake. Instead there should be a broad corridor running between

Opposite Horizontal linkage. Linkage in this Houston, Texas, garden is provided by the wooden bridge, in which simplicity of design is echoed by the simplicity of the valley planting.

Below A fine example of *point de vue.*

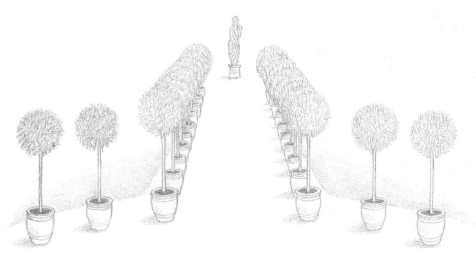

hedge and the rear of any border to which it provides a backdrop. The proportions of a border backed by a wall or hedge also need careful thought. The site may dictate that only a narrow border is possible, but rarely does such a border look anything but mean. The greatest danger with either wall or hedge, however, is that of claustrophobia, for despite the obvious advantages of shelter and privacy, many walls or hedges make one want to escape from the stifling compass of stone or greenery. But this can be avoided by judicious use of openings, archways and see-throughs of various kinds.

When dealing with SLOPES the garden-maker has three choices – to eliminate them somehow, use them as ramps, or build steps to link level with level. Sloping ground was a phenomenon with which the garden architects of the Italian Renaissance became only too familiar. Typically their villas and gardens were sited on a south-facing slope with marvellous views and clear, fresh, healthy air. Here terrace and loggia created the platform while below stretched an area softening into the countryside around. All in all the perfect setting for a bird's-eye view garden with hedging and paths in a strictly formal and dignified setting. But how to link what were in effect extra platforms below the villa? So the garden was conceived as a series of terraces, linked by broad flights of steps and lofty

Opposite left How ideal it would be if the width of every border could conform in harmonious proportion to the height of the wall behind it. Here a low planting would unbalance the design. To compensate, the height of the eremurus in the foreground perfectly marries the vertical and horizontal dimensions.

Red-brick walls are also death to many colour schemes, but here the late Lady Jellicoe, wife of Sir Geoffrey Jellicoe, Britain's foremost garden creater, employed this startling and very effective orange and yellow combination in a garden in Surrey. The varying width of Path and wall border, and varied textures on the further side add a typically individualistic and highly successful touch.

Left Dartington Hall, Devon.

Opposite right An exercise in balanced composition.

Below A slope in a garden can either be terraced, used as a ramp or stepped to link level with level. In this garden in Herefordshire it is intended first to use a steep slope, with complementary planting, while the eye is taken downhill to the focal point vase against the dark background hedge.

hedges. Thus creating a succession of horizontal elements of light and shadow, of shape and form, which added to the grandeur and particularly the unity of the picture.

STEPS should be looked on not only as a means of linking different levels but also a means of drawing a garden together and giving it unity. They can be rustic or formal, plant-edged or balustraded, straight or curving, of uniform width or fanning out towards the bottom – the possibilities for stating or restating the theme of the garden as a whole are almost endless. In material they should be in harmony with other architectural elements in the garden and of course with the house.

As with paths, steps which are too narrow tend to disturb the peace and balance of a layout. A generous width, perhaps approaching that of the terrace to which they give access, is desirable. Another crucial proportion is that between tread and riser. Short-

treaded steps, which may be necessary if the slope is steep, give a sense of hurry; broad treads breathe ease and timelessness. There is a tendency, however, to make the treads too broad in relation to the risers. A complete pace is the ideal width. Anything less, or more, interrupts one's walking rhythm. And it is worth remembering that overhanging treads can create a most useful extra element of shadow – a bonus employed to the full by the garden architects of the Italian Renaissance.

So from the house we have stepped out on to the platform, and from the platform we have been led, by various horizontal devices to . . . what? To a bare field in a single plane setting; an undifferentiated, indeterminate expanse of nothing in particular? Or perhaps to a confusion of half-thought-through and half-hatched schemes, or no scheme at all? Or have we been transported to a special paradise? A garden which bewitches the viewer by its repose and tranquillity, yet one which also holds mystery and excitement? Above all one which soothes the eye and contents the spirit, come summer, come winter.

Opposite Here, in Cornwall, the problem of levels has been solved by the traditional use of stone-faced terracing and distinguished formal steps. In such a setting the planting must be as elegant as the ornamentation if it is not to look incongruous.

Below In order to overcome a very steep slope in this garden in Powys, Wales, a series of terraces covered by intensive herbaceous planting has been created. The terraces are completely hidden and the effect is of a tiered, sloping sea of colour. This is admirably complemented by the stark stone and ironwork.

4 THE VERTICAL DIMENSION

By line, by plummet and unfriendly sheers,
To form with verdure what the builder form'd with stone.
Egregious madness; yet pursu'd
With pains unwearied, and expence unsumm'd,
And science doating. Hence the sidelong walls
Of shaven yew; the holly's prickly arms
Trimm'd into high arcades; the tonsile box
Wove, in mosaic mode of many a curl.[1]

When peace succeeded the frequent bouts of warfare which ravaged Europe for much of the Middle Ages, it became possible to look beyond the fortress garden. The boundary walls of castle and monastery had served both to keep out and to keep in; they screened and protected the inmates from the wild outside while within, they enabled them to create their 'glorietas' – the private paradise – part of their world of exclusivity, of privileged delight. So what had formerly been principally enclosure for defence became division for

A variety of vertical elements in a Houston, Texas, garden which, combined with a modern form of the ancient knot garden, create an exciting effect. The height of the edging and lax trimming cleverly bridges the divide between the starkly geometrical and the natural. It brings a sense of luxuriant formality and creates a series of compartments within which a wide range of planting would be equally at home. The embossing effect could be enhanced by raising the flower beds through lining the inside of the low hedges with boards or plastic sheeting and filling to the brim with soil before planting.

aesthetic purposes as well. The raised mounds, (mounts, or mottes,) which had once served as watchtowers were often embellished with summerhouses to form part of the overall garden design thus becoming platforms from which to gaze on the outside world; while the boundary walls themselves were often crenellated and decorated.

In response to this new outward vision the enclosed boxes which were the legacy of medieval gardens were soon felt to be too constricting. There was need for sub-division but it had to be from something less dominating, from walls of the imagination, divisions which to the eye provided a firm structure, and both created compartments and provided linkage from one part of the garden to another, but on the ground were little more than token walls or boundary markers. These divisions were formed by low evergreen hedges or wooden fencing, often brightly painted, sometimes they were nothing more than edgings made of stone, bones or anything suitable.

Some plants in these ancient gardens, however, demanded a frame on which to grow and these vertical accents made a welcome break to the eye. What more pleasant than to rest on a turfed seat in the shade of a vine-covered arbour, delightfully called a 'shadowe house' and perhaps made of trellis or 'carpenter's work', as it was described, and view one's garden where focal points or view catchers relieved blandness.

For a garden which lacks focus lacks excitement. A flat expanse of nothing in particular is deathly dull and highly unsatisfying. Even startlingly coloured and intricate flower-beds will appear monotonous without some vertical element. And vertical accents are to be found in every style and period of garden history. The Vertical Dimension should be looked upon as a completely separate plane. But one wonders how often those who create gardens truly think on that plane?

'Without which what?' is a phrase which should reverbrate and continue to reverbrate in the head of every garden designer. How often does one come across a perfectly balanced and composed scene. It is a combination that works. One that feels right and gives

'Without Which What?' By hiding with a finger the stone ornament in this garden in Newbury, Berkshire, it is possible to see how significant it is to the whole composition and how without it something special would be lost. We are far more restrained in our use of Garden Ornament than were our gardening ancestors and our gardens are the losers.

There must be a clear and uncluttered line of sight to a focal point or view catcher. This one, in a garden in Ireland, catches the eye both by its verticality and quaint design. It is clearly here for a purpose and the viewer's step is unerringly directed to find out why.

a deep sense of satisfaction. But why does it do so? Why is it so successful? To find this out screen one of the salient features with the palm of the hand. Slowly open the fingers, and close them again. Then will become clear how empty the garden would be without it. How essential it is to the atmosphere and composition of the whole.

Usually such a FOCAL POINT is something precise and definite and in the third dimension – a bush, specimen tree, a piece of topiary or sculpture, pot, tub or urn, a seat or gazebo, a gap in a wall or hedge, or some other design feature. The list is endless, but the purpose is the same, to catch the eye and anchor the scene. However, a focal point need by no means be vertical – it might as easily be a crossway on a path, a change in the pattern of paving, a knot bed, a pool, a curve in an otherwise straight vista. All can catch the eye as effectively as a more vertical accent.

There are many ways to lead the eye towards the focal point – twin hedges or borders, a double row of tubs, a path, avenue or pergola. But whatever the focal point it must be uncluttered, approached by a straight and unhampered line of sight. The eye must never be distracted by colour, shape or design in the foreground. Additionally a focal point must harmonize with other elements in the garden design – in setting, in proportion, in material and in texture. It is clear that the siting of such a significant feature in a garden calls for a great deal of careful thought. For instance, should it be framed in a doorway, flanked by other objects, stand out against a contrasting background so as to play upon the subtle effect of textural contrast, or is it so architecturally significant in itself as to visually dominate its surroundings.

It is believed that the Dutch invented the clairvoie or SEE-THROUGH. In their tight little gardens with meticulous planting and surrounded by thick hedges they must have felt intensely hemmed in. So what better way to create a sense of space than by piercing the boundaries with grilles, grates or windows, which at the same time preserved security. It was a practice – sometimes delightfully described as 'peep views' – which was siezed upon by garden designers across Europe and it is an invaluable addition in helping to create mood in a garden. For pierced walls always hint at something interesting on the other side. Developing that theme further, when grille or clairvoie are enlarged

Left An old chimney pot makes a telling focal point.

they become open doors and, ultimately, when the top is removed, the result is a gap flanked by two walls. Beyond lies vista and prospect and to leave the view unencumbered yet provide the necessary protection from straying animals came the ha-ha.

'We frequently make throughviews, called 'Ah, Ah', wrote the seventeenth-century French garden author Dezalier d'Argenville, 'which are openings in the walls without grills, to the very level of the walks, with a large and deep ditch at the foot of them, lined on both sides to sustain the earth, and prevent the getting over. This surprizes the eye upon coming near it making one cry Ah! Ah! from which it takes its name. This sort of opening is, on some occasions, to be preferred, for that it does not shut up the prospect. . .'[2]

Right Bois de Moutiers, Dieppe, France.

Opposite 'A place of welcome, simplicity and harmony'. (Thomas Church.) All admirably expressed in the design of this entrance to a garden in Fontein Daniel, France. It is not difficult, yet the opportunity so often lost, to arouse a tingle of anticipation by clever entrance planting and show by some sublety of design or layout that this is a place apart.

Below The perfect 'see-through'.

Today the design potential of a gap or door is only half-heartedly exploited. There is a tendency to look on these features as exits, rather than as ENTRANCES as well. Instead of the visitor being 'wowed' visually and aesthetically, made to feel a privileged person entering a new and exciting world, there is a sense of anti-climax. Yet in gardening terms it is simple to emphasize the feature by impact planting, using something visually exciting or strongly scented or both.

Perhaps the most pleasant, and most useful, form of internal wall within a garden is the TRELLIS, 'carpenter's work' as it used to be called. In former days TRELLISWORK was a prime medium for the garden designer, but of all garden constructions this is the most ephemeral, so nothing remains of the magnificent and elaborate confections which graced many a garden in past centuries, save mouthwatering illustrations of an artistic device of great beauty.

Right A simple scene that captures the very essence of the British garden.

The art of the *treillageur* reached its peak in France towards the end of the seventeenth century. From being a purely functional support for plants of a climbing or rambling disposition, *treillage* became an architectural device in its own right and *treillageurs* became honoured members of the gardening fraternity. Their confections became a topic of wonderment and admiration, as well as contributing a most useful form of instant gardening. Visually, trelliswork possesses considerable strength and impact, and in those days it helped serve as compensation for the slim list of flowering plants.

As a 'see-through' trelliswork is unrivalled in providing half-revealing, half-concealing views. The straight lines of strut and upright are satisfying in their own right or as background to climber or creeper. Even in winter, when plant cover has withered, trelliswork makes an interesting statement. It is the ideal medium for creating depth or the illusion of depth in the *trompe l'oeil*. The use of trelliswork as a physical division, but without the dominance or thickness of a wall, hedge or palisade, is a wonderful tool in the hands of any ingenious garden designer. Considering that modern preservatives can weatherproof wood for many years, it is surprising how little use of trelliswork has been made,

Opposite This scene viewed through trelliswork creates a memorable picture. Crucial to the success of this design is the thickness of the trellis batons. Anything more spindly would look mean and insubstantial; if thicker, the impact of the modern knot garden beyond would be reduced.

Right A simple trellis is a fine growing medium for climbing plants.

Far right Trellis used as *trompe l'oeil*.

until recently, especially in view of its value for instant effect, both architectural and decorative. Perhaps the answers lie in its highly labour-intensive manufacture. Our gardens are certainly the poorer for its absence.

In some respects we can look on the PERGOLA, originally a rustic structure for supporting vines, as a near relative of the trellis. As an eighteenth-century writer put it: 'The vines met overhead, forming light corridors, and transpicuous arbours through which the sunbeams play and chequer the shade...'[3] For the pergola also provides division without solid walls, it creates a shady retreat, a framework for growing decorative climbing plants, an invaluable form of linkage and a place to play with shadows.

It was a natural progression from the simple uprights and horizontals of the original pergola to more elaborate supporting and roofing structures – brick or stone arches connected by wooden beams, pillars with wooden cross members, columns and vaults made of trellis or wrought iron. Two quite distinct effects can be perceived here: lightness and airiness, or, the airless,

Trelliswork. By bracing the trellis away from the wall a sense of depth can be created and clever angling of the batons can focus attention on a central object or ornament in a way which is difficult to achieve with any other medium. Trelliswork was formerly exploited in the seventeenth and eighteenth centuries in elaborate and exciting ways (partly to compensate for the much reduced plant palette of the day). As perhaps the easiest form of the instant gardening we seek today, and certainly one of the most effective ways of providing a vertical element quickly, it is surprising that we do not make greater use of this exciting medium.

'The whole is a place to tarry with secure delight, or to saunter with perpetual amusement.' (Thomas Whateley.) This pergola in Ravello, Italy, shows how this basic structure in the evolution of garden design developed from a simple, rustic support for vines. Here is a shady retreat, a division without solid walls, an invaluable means of linkage and a place to play with shadows.

Through repetition, avenues or allées have the power to draw the eye down their length. Planting can provide many permutations: close planting increases the sense of tension and hurry and, sometimes mystery; conversely, more distant planting creates a sense of ease and tranquillity. Obvious gaps, as here on the right, arouse a sense of curiosity. In addition, cross arches can be used to give an illusion of length, while impact planting, either through tone or form (as in this garden in Barnsley, Gloucestershire) at the near end helps achieve the same effect. A picture which repays close study.

rather claustrophic effect of a tunnel. The pergola proper, with its widely spaced verticals rhythmically framing a succession of views, is a pleasant place to linger in. The tunnel, achieved with a closer spacing of verticals and a thicker cladding of foliage, is a place to hurry through. It pays to be aware of these two possible sensations when planning a covered walk of any kind. To an extent the avenue is a compromise between the two.

In an AVENUE the strong pair of converging lines and the rhythmic repetition of uprights, or their shadows, draw the eye down the main vista. When the uprights are close together a tunnel effect is created, conversely, generous spacing gives a sense of ease. The eye can be influenced, too, by the relative height and spacing of the uprights and by the width of the central axis. In addition, the nature of the underplanting can add to the illusion – heavy planting at the near end gives an impression of greater length, conversely solid planting at the far end appears to shorten the vista. Other perspective tricks include arresting the eye by a centrally placed ornament or the judicious siting of an arch or bridge.

The origins of the RAISED BORDER, a device long used to lend interest to a flat plane garden, go back into the mists of garden creation. The castle gardener soon discovered that by raising up the soil within retaining walls it was possible to make a garden even on solid rock. What is more, most plants benefitted from the improved drainage. The turf seats enjoyed by our ancestors and such an important feature in medieval gardens were also in effect, raised beds; they were planted with sweet-smelling camomile, thyme and other herbs as well as grass. Today, however, the design and planting potential of the raised border is underused. The pronounced horizontal lines add crisp edges and strong shadows while the low retaining wall offers scope for crevice plants, to say nothing of the fact that it is infinitely more pleasurable to garden on a raised bed than on a flat one.

How stereotyped our gardens have become. From time to time we tiptoe towards exciting nonconformity, but hesitantly. Yet in the pages of garden history are to be found many devices, a lot of them in the vertical dimension, which by applying modern horticultural practices and using a plant repertoire the envy of our forebears, we could with greater imagination adopt to

Left Edzell Castle, Scotland.

Opposite The raised bed is a device going back into the mists of garden creation. Here the retaining walls provide homes for a wealth of wall and crevice plants.

Below An ingenious way to deal with a corner.

The use of growing view catchers, architectural plants used to attract attention (by size, colour, leaf form or perhaps sheer improbability) injects an exciting variety into what can otherwise be a terrible sameness.

beautify our gardens. Perhaps we should talk now not only of 'the poet's feeling' and 'the painter's eye' but also of the sculptor's hand!

The PYRAMID is one such. A pyramid, or for that matter a column festooned with climbing plants, a dimly seen foundation through a luxuriance of flower or foliage, affords a vertical accent of exciting, but still rarely used potential.

The TRAINED FRUIT TREE is another example. Almost the only variants to the conventional are the goblet, occasionally, the low cordon, dubbed the 'step-over', and the *arcure*, which now rejoices in the name of 'festoon'. The more elaborate but highly decorative designs favoured during the last century, particularly in France, are almost never seen. They require years of devoted tying and trimming and perhaps we nowadays lack the patience, or is it the imagination?

For not only decorative in their own right, as accents, see-through barriers, providing variety against a host of backgrounds, they were also highly productive. Almost by chance, it appears, we have recently discovered that

Left What nicer way to inject a 'hard' vertical feature into a garden?

Below Clematis are normally looked upon as climbing plants. But in this Herefordshire garden it can be seen that they are admirable scramblers as well. This is 'Beauty of Worcester', a large-flowered mid-season variety.

bending down fruit tree shoots for what was imagined to be an ornamental purpose also has a significant effect on fruit production. But in aesthetic terms where but in France would we find such an admirable combination of beauty with utility?

Normally too we build our WALLS with stones placed one on top of the other and so displaying them in section. Yet what scope there is in colour and texture if they were allowed to face a slope, in effect forming vertical paving.

Another example of an unexploited source lies in WALL AND ROOF GARDENING. The latter customarily means gardening on a roof, never gardening UNDER the roof? Our hanging baskets are generally half or quarter spheres. Why? Window boxes customarily hang beneath a window, but they would be as effective, if not more so, were they hung on a wall or against any upright surface as in many a patio in warmer climes? By not doing this we deprive ourselves of a great deal of

possible vertical effect and simple design satisfaction.

Formerly the watering of hanging baskets was a major disadvantage, but this is no longer the case. So why do we confine ourselves to single hanging baskets? Why not stepped tiers or candelabras of colour and delight? What a joy they would be and a pleasant alternative to the vertical accent so often provided in municipal planting.

Although the vertical dimension has such exciting potential in a garden, and one where the exhortation, 'Be free, be various' is particularly appropriate (words which should be inscribed in letters one foot (30 cm) high above the door of every garden designer), it is also a passport to restlessness in design. Accents, features and exclamation marks should be used sparingly and with reticence, rather than with the liberality so common today. They should contribute to the overall unity of the composition not disturb it.

The construction of most walls ensures that one only sees the constituent stones in section. These paving stones have been placed on a slope to display their upper surface textures. The pink oriental poppy beneath a diervilla in full flower makes a simple but powerful association.

5 BONES

It is interesting, although hardly surprising, that pictures of medieval and cloister gardens rarely show the scene in winter. These were essentially spring, summer and autumn gardens. Come winter only bare stems and dead leaves remained, chilly reminders of human mortality. One can visualize the 'goodlye ladye' of Chaucer's day, walking in her castle garden in winter gazing on an orderly arrangement of neat beds interspersed with trellis, fountains and other all-season ornaments, but little else.

In the cold and damp of winter in a temperate climate the garden can be an unwelcoming place. For most of us, though, our gardens remain visible in winter whether we like it or not. Nevertheless, even when plants are in hibernation a garden can still be a place of peace and delight, although of a different order to that enjoyed in other seasons, for there are still elements that retain interest and pleasure. The crispness of the air can be matched by the crispness of outline, while the etching of some feature against a

The gaunt, skeletal effect of the leafless avenue and distant line of poplars is the very essence of the winter scene in a temperate climate – as here in Provence, France. If your garden design can withstand winter scrutiny when the 'bones' are no longer hidden by flower or foliage, then there cannot be much wrong with it. Here we can appreciate the true bones of this garden – the textural contrast between the yew hedge, the lawns and the paving. As the Garden Trinity – evergreenery, stone and water – provided the backbone to the gardens of Rome, Islam and Renaissance Italy, so it does to the all-season garden. Greater textural contrast could be created by varying the height of the lawn cut.

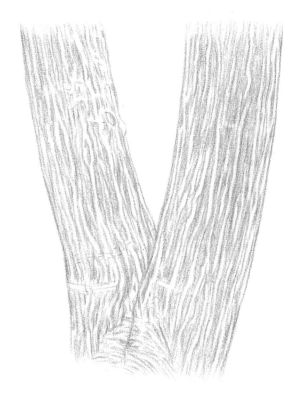

Left Bark striations.

white background, or the tracery of branches silhouetted against a leaden sky, is the very essence of the winter scene. In the bleakness, glimpses of colour are particularly welcome – colour from the few berries left by the birds, occasional shafts of an almost alien sunlight illuminating the striations of bark or picking out the subtle tones of lichen-covered stones, the adventitious winter flower burrowing up through frost and snow.

Overall though it can be a depressing scene, still water in particular presenting a dull and dismal appearance. Yet a snow-covered garden has such a sense of blanketted peace that one almost feels compelled to talk in whispers. Wintertime is the real test of a garden design for now the skeleton, the 'bones', are fully visible and no longer fleshed by flowers or foliage. If your design can withstand this winter scrutiny there cannot be much wrong with the basic structure, and the principal elements in that patterned structure are the Garden Trinity – Evergreenery, Stone and Water (the latter deserving a chapter of its own, Chapter 7).

EVERGREENS were, and are, the living bones of the winter garden. Most contribute a vertical element and traditionally they created the boundary for the knot garden and the more elaborate parterre. This ancient form of carpet bedding coloured in summer, pure pattern in winter, was intended to be viewed from

above to be properly appreciated. The French diarist Saint-Simon, who took a jaundiced view of the patterned parterre garden of the day, declared that it was perfect for housemaid's viewing the scene from the upper floors!

Particularly impressive were the intricate parterre designs perfected by the Mollet family in France in the 1640s. These have the charm of sumptuous tapestry and bewitch by their sworls and swoops. For modern taste such extravagant designs are over-elaborate and too distracting. Nevertheless, this style does have its uses, especially when a parterre is intended to catch the eye, rather than harmonize with the whole composition.

The disciplined charm of knots and parterres with their virtually flat, embossed two-dimensional image is particularly effective in drawing a garden together and imposing a sense of formality. In lesser form a solid edge, from trimmed grass, paving, a raised bed, low wall or a hedge, emphasizes and draws the attention in the same way that a carefully chosen frame enhances a picture.

In summer this picture can be bright with flowers, but in winter the colour must come from evergreens or from infills of coloured pebbles, gravels or sand. But there is the ever-present danger in this type of garden of over-elaboration. As a French visitor was heard to

exclaim on seeing a vulgarly ostentatious recreation of a coat-of-arms in a Scottish garden, 'C'est magnifique, mais ce n'est pas un jardin!'[1]

The story of the ebb and flow of enthusiasm for evergreens over the years is as fascinating as the warring over the 'formal' and 'natural' schools of gardening which so preoccupied our gardening ancestors. The term 'evergreen' of course now embraces the ever-silver, the ever-gold, the ever-yellow and the ever-grey, as well as a host of intermediate tones besides.

The Romans and the Islamic gardeners of Southern Spain had a wide range of evergreenery to choose from, but in northern climes the choice was more circum-scribed. Box, yew and juniper were the common

options. There was also the gawky Scots pine, the only conifer indigenous to the British Isles. This had its enthusiasts and its detractors, though few went so far as Sir William Temple who damned everyone who chose 'the race of pine' as 'erroneous' and 'witless'. Indeed conifers continue to divide the loyalities of the garden-ing world as much as heathers – one is either an Ericarean, or one is not. But if Sir William could see the immense range of colour and growth available in conifers today, and the scope for textural contrast that they con-tribute to a garden, he might have revised his opinions.

Conifers are by no means the only natural all-season plants available. In temperate climates many deciduous plants retain some leaf colour or form and remain at least partially evergreen except in the severest winters. Others contribute splendid bark colour or striations the year through. And it is sometimes forgotten how decorative in their skeletal survival can be twig, leaf or the remnants of flowers or seed pods.

But it is with TOPIARY that most of us associate growing bones. In general terms topiary is defined as the practice of clipping and trimming plants into unnatural forms. Under this broad head come neatly clipped borders; fine architectural hedges; geometrically shaped trees, shrubs and other plants; animal and human figures; and sometimes quite amazing freestyle fantastical shapes.

When Pope, Addison and others turned their scorn and fury on the formal style of gardening, their fullest wrath was turned on topiary, the derided 'tonsured greenery'. Pope, in particular, enjoyed himself hugely. He invented a 'Virtuoso Gardiner who has a Turn for Sculpture' and would readily cut 'Family Pieces of Men,

Opposite left In this garden in Gloucestershire the background evergreen hedge and shaped box designs provide all-season interest. Topiary, once over-used and later derided as 'tonsured greens', is making a determined comeback into today's garden design as its value as bridge between the harsh straight lines of architecture and lax natural growth becomes better appreciated.

Opposite right A classic parterre – the formal garden of France.

Above left An all-season picture of great charm and strength.

Left Topiary on the grand scale.

Women and Children. Any Ladies that please may have their Effigies in Myrtle, and their Husbands in Horn beame.' Among this worthy's stock was

Adam and Eve in yew. Adam a little shattered by the fall of the tree of knowledge in the great storm, Eve and the Serpent very flourishing.
The Tower of Babel, not yet finished.
St. George in box. His arm scarce long enough, but will be in condition to stick the dragon by next April.
A pair of giants, stunted, to be sold cheaply.
Divers eminent modern poets in bays, somewhat blighted, to be disposed of, a pennyworth.
A quickset hog, shot up into a porcupine, by its being forgot one week in rainy weather.
Noah's Ark in holly, standing on the Mount, the ribs a little damaged for want of water.[2]

Although in Pope's time, the early 1700s, Holland was considered to be the home of topiary, the practice seems to have migrated there from Italy via France. But in Holland the topiarist's art was brought to perfection, the tiny scale of the average Dutch garden of that time precluding any but the smallest free-growing trees.

Below Magnificent 'bones'.

The practice of clipping and trimming growing trees into unnatural shapes, *ars tonsilis*, probably began in Roman times. In design terms this living sculpture provided a bridge between the solid construction of architecture and that of growing plants. In the gardens of the philosopher Pliny clipped hedges and shaped greenery were an essential element and, to a considerable extent, substituted for flowers. Although slow-growing and not always popular – one writer referred to it as 'a melancholy, smelly green'[3] – box was the common stock, but great ingenuity was also shown in the shaping of citrus, cypress, myrtle and such scramblers as honeysuckle, jasmine and ivy.

Although the Dark Ages wiped out all but the vestiges of the gardens of the Roman Empire, topiary was pursued with even greater verve and imagination in the Middle Ages. Many varieties of trees were trimmed, trained and twisted into growing architectural features of great charm – intricate mazes, arbours made of pleached or intertwined branches, green tunnels, even complete tree-houses. Lime trees in particular were popular, and often turned into two- or even three-storied constructions. Low hedges were sculpted of lavender, rosemary and other sweet-smelling herbs. Green walls were created of yew, privet and sweetbriar, and of hornbeam, which was particularly popular in Holland. Much ingenuity was devoted to the making of 'privie ways', which allowed the ladies of the house to walk privately and in shade; into this category came the *herber* or hedge running the length of a wall, and the *gallerie*, a more elaborate affair of pleached branches parted at intervals to make 'windows' so that its occupants might 'more fully view and have delight of the whole beautie of the garden'.[4] Occasionally these sheltered walks housed 'roosting places' where the visitor might rest and linger. Most elaborate of all and giving the greatest scope to the highly inventive gardeners of the day was the garden house, pleached bower or arbour, entirely made of living greenery, although this was sometimes supported with trellis during the growing stage.

Topiary has always had its critics. In the early 1600s Francis Bacon wrote: 'I, for my part, do not like images cut in juniper or other garden stuff – they be for children'.[5] For others it is precisely the fantasy of topiary images which appeals: 'Your gardener can frame your lesser wood to the shape of men armed in the field,

Green textures. The close-cropped ivy provides the perfect background to this bronze relief. Against this simple but hugely effective set piece anything but an equally dignified foreground planting scheme would look wildly out of place. But in winter the composition would still be powerful.

Planting grass or other evergreen subjects between bricks or paving is a useful addition to the all-season palette, but the practice, which would be as useful in a small as a large garden, is rarely seen. This is in a garden in Ravello, Italy.

Right A tranquil well-balanced
scene.

ready to give battle: of swift running Grey-hounds, or of well-sented and true running Hounds to chase the Deer or hunt the Hare. This kind of hunting shall not waste your Corn nor much your Coyne.'[6]

The overuse of topiary, 'tonsured clutter' it has been called, in the style of the eighteenth-century Dutch garden, can be overwhelming. Yet, when used with restraint, it is an immensely effective medium, and a versatile one too, for it can provide robust structure as well as ornament all year round. Topiary of course takes time, so it runs counter to the modern 'instant' approach to gardening.

In the gardens of the past GARDEN ORNAMENT supplied many of the deficiencies of a limited plant palette. Most of the flowers planted were indigenous spring and early summer flowers, thus without special treatment beds and borders would be bare for much of the year. As we have seen evergreens and topiary principally

provided the living bones, the non-growing elements consisted of stonework, statues, urns, fountains, containers of all kinds, fences, trellis, patterned paths, and so on.

Le Grand Siècle of Louis XIV was a heyday of garden ornament, an era of massive fountains, balustrades, grottoes, trelliswork of amazing complexity and architectural magnificence. The garden 'pictures' of the eighteenth century called for busts, urns, temples and follies. The Victorians, in their muddled yearning for a bit of everything, were passionately fond of garden ornaments – artificial chamois on artificial mountains, extravaganzas of wrought iron, pretty glasshouses, marvellous cast-iron fountains, romantic hermitages, sometimes complete with stuffed hermit . . . .

However, the accolade for the most imaginative use of garden ornament must go to the seventeenth-century Dutch. In this chequerboard land dissected by

Our fruit and vegetable gardens in winter often resemble steeplechase courses, and not even interesting steeplechase courses at that. In this potager in a garden in Barnsley, Gloucestershire, the blending of utility and decoration is finely displayed. The arches seen here as supports for marrows and gourds, as well as varied fruit-tree training elsewhere in the garden, provide a continuing structural interest the year round.

All season tracery provided by fruit-tree training.

canals and swept by wind they developed a style which depended on geometric beds and elaborate decoration – a world of coloured pebbles and sand, painted tree trunks to match the gaily painted shutters of their houses and bushes fashioned into quaint and throughly unnatural shapes. Any and every device was used to relieve the monotony of a flat landscape, punctuated only by a church spire or avenue of poplars.

But now that our plant palette is so much larger, why should we need to resort to plant substitutes? Coloured glass balls and discs to catch the sunlight, little bells, wind harps, miniature figures in miniature landscapes . . . all of these pleased our gardening predecessors but they are anathema to most of us, as out of place as Christmas decoration in high summer.

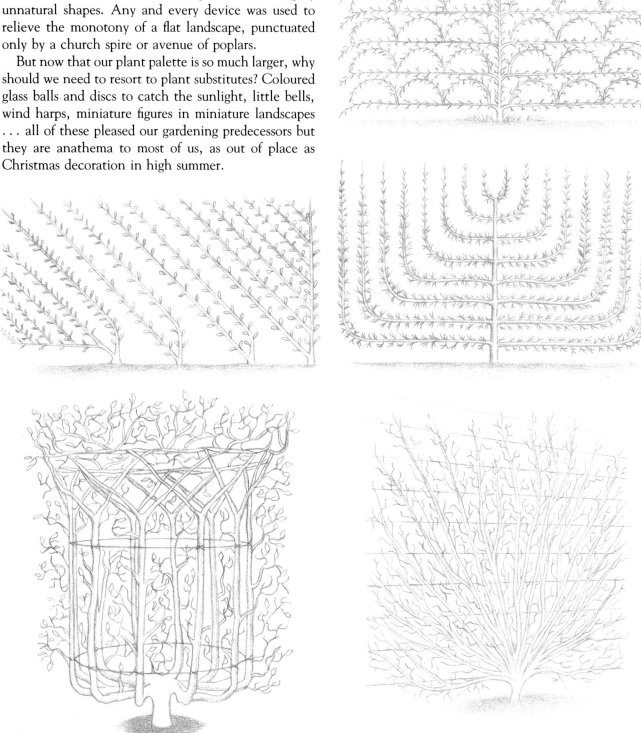

But are we right to spurn them? Any child on a second visit to a garden offering sparkling mobiles and chiming bells would make unhesitatingly for such conceits and stand entranced. Why? Because they are different, 'various' as ancient garden writers urged gardeners to be. They capture much of what we are trying to achieve in our gardens, although they are not something which we, with all our accumulated prejudices, call 'gardening'.

Perhaps the time has come for us to search our souls and ask ourselves if the path of our own exquisite taste may not be paved with more than a little bias if not a little hypocrisy? After all the garden gnome has a noble ancestry!

Already we are injecting, perhaps unconsciously, a host of artificial conceits into our gardens. It would be hard, for instance, to conceive of anything less natural than a pole with a basket of flowers hanging from it, unless one likens it to an epiphytic growth on a tree trunk in some tropical paradise. Yet we cheerfully accept hanging baskets as a legitimate part of garden-

ing, and immensely colourful and decorative they are too. So what is permissible and what is not, for these features are perennial in the truest sense of the word.

The cost of real stone is prohibitive, so we turn to plastic or reconstituted stone substitutes – quite permissible. Topiary designs, provided they are not too small and there are not too many of them – permissible. Anything smacking of a human figure made of modern materials – lead, stone and bronze excepted – not permissible. High glaze patterned pots and plant containers, preferably with some real or supposed ethnic origin – permissible. And so on. One has only to go to a garden centre today and cast a quizzical eye over the wares on display to see that today's interpretation of garden 'taste' is riddled with inconsistencies and contradictions, and this applies to the practical as well as the ornamental wares. When we put up green-plastic-covered trellis on our walls we visualize it covered with luxuriant flowers and leaves; we conveniently forget that from November to March we will be stuck with the thing, in all its incongruity.

6 A MIXED BORDER

What strands shall fom the Carpet of Desire?
Mixed strands, from every land a ray
Shall weave the Beauty to which all aspire. [1]

By the Victorian era, the violent pendulum swings between the formal and informal schools of gardening were beginning to settle. There is a tremendous feeling of excitement about this period in gardening evolution. It was a time of explosion in gardening popularity as cheap printing coincided with the commercial and domestic affluence of the burgeoning middle classes who began to turn their considerable energies to their

gardens. A ready market and easier travel encouraged plant explorers, sponsored by the newly created Horticultural Society (later to become the Royal Horticultural Society), the botanic gardens at Kew and by the larger nurseries, to scour the world for new and exciting specimens to feed the growing enthusiasms, particularly the collecting of such exotic species as orchids.

In garden design, although eclecticism was the

Right Modern carpet bedding. Victorian-style carpet bedding dominated Nature as surely as previous formal styles. Not until William Robinson, a little over a century ago, started his crusade were the shackles of that convention broken. These beds, in a Hertfordshire garden, however, can be seen as transitional between true carpet bedding and the island-type beds which Robinson himself advocated.

Opposite Springtime in Herefordshire. A woodland garden after the heart of William Robinson, who popularized so many of our current practices in cultivation and garden design.

prevailing mode, the trend, which satisfied both vanity as well as taste, was for ultra-formal bedding schemes using half-hardy 'exotics', raised by the tens of thousands in greenhouses across the land.

But something was missing. It was fun to show off, to grow more and better and different half-hardy plants, but the garish, strutting regimental rows had a horrid sameness about them. And when, after five months of splendour, these plants, or whatever followed in a successional planting scheme, had to be lifted and their beds dug over, the legacy was bare earth as gaunt and forlorn as any ballroom after the dancers have gone. What had become of the balanced, restful garden that seemed to most satisfy man's craving? Instead of the peaceful expression of the sinuous curve which seduced and enticed the walker ever deeper into the magic, secret world of the garden, here was brash rigid uniformity, the geometry of straight lines and regular curves and all open to the gaze at the same time.

Though order and discipline were the essence of the style of living enjoyed by the Victorians, now, secure and confident, they began to seek another less ordered outlet for their imaginations and their gardens. The answer was on their own doorsteps and in another sort of garden, the cottage garden with its riot of traditional flowers – pinks, pansies, marigolds, hollyhocks and roses, especially the roses. Many country gardens had gone on in much the same way for centuries, caring little for passing fashion and even less for form.

Additionally, many of the plants then becoming available, either through plant hunting or plant breeding were unsuited to cultivation in formal beds; on the other hand, they were too fine and sometimes too delicate to be banished to the rough and tumble of life in the wild garden. Hence there was a need for a planting style somewhere between the rigid uniformity of massed planting, the delightful anarchy of the cottage garden, the shrubbery (which had partly evolved to display collections of trees and shrubs) and the 'wildness' of uncultivated ground. In particular there was no place for perennial herbaceous subjects and the less rumbustious shrubs. It was the dawn of the MIXED BORDER.

William Robinson (1839–1935) is chiefly remembered as the champion of the 'Wild Garden', by which he meant a garden in which hardy exotic plants (plants

foreign to Britain) could thrive naturally, without constant care, rather than the embellished woodland with its undertones of wilderness which the name implies today – he has been widely misquoted and misunderstood on this point. But to William Robinson must also go much of the credit for creating the forerunner of today's mixed border in order to cater for the influx of new and exciting hardy plants. But he was really beholden to a much older practice.

It is now beginning to emerge that the Landscape School, far from being the universal arbiter of gardening taste in England through much of the latter half of the eighteenth century, really only affected the larger parks and richer landowners. The gardens of those with smaller houses and smaller means were almost unaffected; in these gardens flowers continued to dominate, as they always had. As more work is being put into the study of the history of gardening design it is emerging that by the first half of the eighteenth century considerable use was being made of irregular planting patterns. These sometimes took the shape of mixed plantings of clumps of herbaceous plants at the foot of trees or shrubs, as at Strawberry Hill, the home of Horace Walpole. Elsewhere, garden owners sought something other than symmetry, and sinuous lines were by no means uncommon. So Sir William Chambers' 'Chinese' conceptions, introduced in the last decades of the eighteenth century, may not have been as revolutionary as once supposed. Here he is, talking about successional planting and the use of colour:

> . . . avoid all sudden transitions, both with regard to dimension and colour; rising gradually from the smallest flowers to hilli-ocks, paeonies, sun-flowers, carnation-poppies, and others of the boldest growth; and varying their tints, by easy gradation, from white, straw-colour, purple and incarnate, to the deepest blues, and most brilliant crimsons and scarlets . . . to dark and gloomy colours they [the 'Chinese'] oppose such as are brilliant and to complicated forms simple ones, distributing by judicious arrangement, the different masses of light and shade, in such a manner as to render the composition at once distinct in the parts, and striking in the whole . . . In large plantations, the flowers generally grow in the natural ground: but in flower gardens and all other parts that are highly

Modern cottage garden planting. A magnificent riot of colour in a Dorset, Vermont, garden. At first sight this may appear casual, even accidental and to lack form. That is a delusion for a great deal of care and deliberation, art and flair, go into the making of such a border.

Left Viewpoint 1. Only a passing bird could see these superbly colourful borders in their entirety (in Hampshire, home of the late Sir Cecil Beaton). By refusing to be restricted to the customary planting of 'tallest at the back, shortest to the front', a miniature landscape of great charm and visual impact has been created. But the narrow path means that we are in fact looking at an unfolding scenario no wider than thirty degrees to either side. Thus the border plantings completely hide whatever lies beyond them.

Opposite Viewpoint 2. This border at Blickling Hall, Norfolk, a property of the English National Trust, is best seen from a distance. By standing back, the magnificence, and the detail, of this border can be taken in with a single sweep of the eye, and clearly bold groupings are most effective.

kept, they are in pots buried in the ground: which as fast as the bloom goes off, are removed, and others are brought to supply their places; so that there is a constant succession for almost every month of the year, and the flowers are never seen, but in the height of their beauty. . .[2]

It is interesting to note that Gertrude Jekyll, a century later, also advocated colours in harmony rather than contrast, and that planting in pots, for easy removal after flowering, was a practice followed in Le Nôtre's day.

A significant garden in the evolution of the border was at Nuneham Courtenay near Oxford. This was created around 1780 for the 2nd Earl Harcourt as a symbolic garden dedicated among others to the philosopher Rousseau and his concept of perfect nature. Rousseau, as one of his supporters described, had sought to bring 'the natural garden to men who had only walked between tonsured yews and rectilinear flower borders.'[3] This was a garden intended to be 'perceived and felt', to recreate the 'complete experience' of the Italian Renaissance garden. It was constructed as a 'pilgrim route', so that the visitor should experience a rising crescendo of emotions as he made his way round the course, pausing on his way to absorb a succession of visual experiences, until coming face to face with a statue of the great Rousseau himself. Were he to find difficulty finding the right emotion, a guidebook helped him on his way. 'Check the useful tear', he was urged at

Nuneham Park, Oxfordshire.

one pausing point. 'Strike the forehead in the dust' at another. This garden had long since vanished when William Robinson came on the scene but one cannot help wondering how that short-tempered Irishman would have reacted to such instructions!

Though Robinson's soul might not have been as up-lifted as some, he would certainly have recognized the merits of the planting system at Nuneham Courtenay, which he was later to adopt. The designer of this garden was the Reverend William Mason who immortalized his planting concepts in his extremely long poem *The English Garden*:

> So here did Art arrange her flow'ry groups
> Irregular, yet both in patches quaint
> But interpos'd between the wand'ring lines
> Of shaven turf which twisted to the path.[4]

But whether innovatory or adapted and refined from past practice, Robinson was responsible for publicizing what we would today recognize as the mixed border. His purpose in this was to incorporate permanent flowers which were hardy and, as he put it, 'of the highest order of beauty'.[5] By present standards the plant repertoire in Robinson's day was small, although growing fast, and this may explain his decision to incorporate shrubs to add interest.

'Verdure' and 'repose' were his two watchwords. By 'verdure' Robinson meant exuberant growth and by 'repose', enough room for the full expression of each plant, each bed and each group in his planting schemes. It would appear from his directions that in order to allow sufficient repose his planting was wider apart than we would normally allow today, the gaps being filled with bulbs, principally lilies. He planted in groups, varying sizes and shapes, 'holding some apart and some together by "turfing" plants beneath and spaces of repose around, letting other groups merge into one another, suitable plants intermingling.'[6]

His 'turfing', or what we would recognize as ground-cover, consisted of violas, pinks and other low plants, especially stonecrops, which he found ideal for 'paving' and 'carpeting' the ground. These created, as he put it, 'little lawns' between the larger plants in a bed or border, many of which were all-season and provided winter interest as well.

However instructive his approach was, he found himself faced with the conundrum of how best to view his borders. He deplored the then, and often present trend: 'Gardeners', he declared, 'seldom look at general effects or at the whole of things. The flowers are so dear to them that the garden, as a picture, is left to chance, and hence so much ugliness in gardens, for those at least who look to the robe as more than the buttons.'[7]

The problem of viewing a border which runs parallel to a path or wall, or of viewing parallel borders with a narrow path between them, is that it is only really possible to see thirty degrees or so to either side, widening to 180 degrees if it is possible to stand back far enough. Usually, one looks at a border 'in the long', enjoying as one proceeds along it a gradually unfolding picture with a narrow but ever-changing focus. This linear scenario dictates the general form of planting, which is often one of dreadful sameness, with short plants at the front and tall plants at the back. This has the effect of making an already narrow bed appear even narrower. As the general grizzle of gardeners is that borders are too narrow, such a planting system is clearly self-defeating and compounds the problem.

In the mass, however, the linear border can be spectacular, but at the expense of being able to admire the individual beauty of its constituents. Robinson's solution was to create separate, irregular WALK-ROUND BEDS (which sound uncommonly like what we refer to as island beds), in which height was an important consideration. These could be seen and admired from all sides, 'in the round', as it were. He avoided one of his pet hates, a set pattern which wearied the eye, and produced instead 'quiet grace and verdure and little pictures month by month'.[8]

Robinson's walk-round beds contained a catholic mix of shrubs – to provide bulk and height and prolong the season – together with perennials and lilies. 'This', he wrote with some glee, 'destroyed all set pattern [what is sometimes referred to as "pastrycook gardening"] to such an extent that it was impossible for the eye to take in the arrangement or contents of any single bed from one standpoint'. Then he adds, 'While the arrangement of a geometrical garden is seen at a glance, it was here necessary to walk round each bed to acquaint oneself with the contents.'[9] Within these walk-round beds Robinson clearly had the greatest fun as he played with the six elements of plant association – COLOUR, HEIGHT, SHAPE, TEXTURE, TONE and SEASON.

Essentially he was introducing plants with diverse growth, foliage, tone and texture as a foil to brilliant colours. Perhaps here we can see an early example of what could be termed DIFFUSION PLANTING where wispy foliage or flowers act as a thin veil over a more substantial body of colour or form.

Some of his resulting plant associations must have been spectacular considering the limited range of plants at his disposal. One of the most successful, and which gave him particular pleasure was rhododendrons inter-planted with unstaked 'star flowers' (michaelmas daisies, asters). These were one of the latest importations from America and being widely hybridized, as one of the most welcome herbaceous season-stretchers in many a year. According to Robinson, if some kinds were dwarfed by their neighbouring shrubs it did not lessen their value but rather increased it, as it helped to produce varieties of tone, and destroyed the common way of 'setting plants to a face, as if one were laying bricks'.[10] To his mind they created a 'broken and beautiful instead of a monotonous surface'.[11]

Unlike other art forms a garden is a changing medium. When plants grow they have the tiresome and disconcerting habit of not growing uniformly thus throwing into disarray the original proportions the designer had in mind, proportion in relation to neigh-bouring plants or with the broader setting. As a garden is also essentially a personal creation it is little wonder that the replication of an old garden seldom works, not least because the background and structural bones may have grown out of scale. Although a copy may be as true to the original as research, care and love can make it, there can never be the perfect recapturing of the precise content, style and atmosphere of the original. Inevitably, it is only an interpretation.

This is why attempts to replicate Gertrude Jekyll's borders never quite succeed. They often fail to capture the mood she was trying to create, that of a garden 'fashioned into a dream of beauty, a place of perfect rest and refreshment of mind and body – a series of soul-satisfying pictures – a treasure of well-set jewels'.[12] She recognized that one of the chief charms of the cottage garden was scale. Expand a cottage garden on a larger canvas and it looks an incongruous mess. Her genius was to transpose the essence of the cottage garden into the refined, sophisticated form of the herbaceous and mixed borders we know today.

Miss Jekyll's planting was not in blocks, or groups or splodges, but in drifts and swathes and sweeps. This gave a sense of vitality and movement to her creations, so the eye was continuously and unconsciously taken onward to some point of focus. Further, gaps were never left after some variety had passed its best. This was the key to her superb successional planting. The key to her overall planting was to 'place every plant or group of plants with such care and definite intention that they shall form part of an harmonious whole'.[13]

It is readily accepted that the partnership between Gertrude Jekyll and the young architect Edwin Lutyens (1869–1944) was seminal in the evolution of modern gardening design, characterized by the successful marriage of architecture and planting. What is less generally recognized is that Gertrude Jekyll's earlier and long-standing friendship and association with Robinson – she succeeded him as editor of his magazine – was equally significant. Together they popularized planting concepts which are still as valid today as they ever were. Their declared intent was to loosen the 'bondage of fashion which had even driven ... the good old border flowers out of the little cottage plot'.[14] They saw contemporary gardens as having 'no thought; no arrangement; no bold groupings; no little pictures made with living colours; no variety; no contrast but mere repetition'.[15]

Like all gardeners, Gertrude Jekyll found herself in the unavoidable dilemma that borders need to be seen from a distance as well as close to. To overcome the tendency of ending up with a gradually unrolling carpet of flowers she included dot plants of different heights among her 'textured masses', thus creating a series of landscapes in miniature. To add substance to the border, she raised the planting at each end; this had a foreshortening effect on what can otherwise become a long, narrow strip. For the most part, however, she was disinclined, at least in her earlier gardens, to employ non-herbaceous subjects except as background, and was content to let one area play its course after which attention turned to another part of the garden, a luxury few of us have the space for today.

Robinson also constructed his walk-round beds as landscapes in miniature, but he looked on them as pro-viding a continuity of colour, everchanging but always with something to attract attention. He employed far greater height variation than did Gertrude Jekyll in her

Monoculture. These blue delphiniums in a garden in Ireland seen against the background hedge create an architectural impression which would be wholly lost with a more fussy arrangement.

early years and never hesitated to use non-herbaceous plants to extend both interest and season. Today there is a trend towards walk-round beds not so much as features in themselves but as frames for other views in the garden. This gives a much-needed vitality to what can easily become a static and complacent picture. It also provides an additional change of focus, so important in bringing interest to garden design.

More or less since the end of the Second World War the HERBACEOUS BORDER in its true magnificence has been considered dead, mortally wounded by the high cost of upkeep, except in privileged gardens. The labour involved in successional planting and maintenance and the overwhelming disadvantage in temperate climates of patches of bare earth in winter has gradually pushed gardeners in the direction of the mixed border and the all-season evergreen and conifer border. But a resurgence may be imminent. It is now possible to suppress weeds and keep the soil moist by covering the earth with a permeable (geotextile) membrane hidden by wood chips, peat, bark or a sprinkling of soil. In short, it is now possible to create an almost no-upkeep

Yet shall the graceful line
  forget to please,
If border'd close by sidelong
  parallels,
Nor only mixt with those
  opposing curves
That give the charm of
  contrast. (Sir William
  Temple.)

Monoculture. These twin strips
of impatiens complement the
simplicity of the architecture,
trees, hedge and sweep of lawn
in a Southampton garden, on
the Long Island shoreline.

Fruit Salad Planting – but immensely colourful nevertheless. The soft-toned irregular Cotswold stone is ideally suited to luxuriant planting within a firm structure as in this garden in Gloucestershire.

border to give maximum impact for minimum effort, the ideal all gardeners seek.

Another 'border' precedent of considerable interest to the modern gardener is mentioned in Sir William Chambers' *A Dissertation on Oriental Gardening*. In this he wrote that his 'Chinese' handled their herbaceous plants in a manner quite unlike anything he had seen before; instead of planting in groups, beds or borders, they went in for dot planting, the dots being of handsome size as several different plants were placed in the same hole, so that foliage and flowers mingled. Thus it was possible with minimum effort to produce in one spot a medley of colour, form, tone, texture and seasonal interest. This is quite contrary to Robinson's

call for repose which advocated that each plant be allowed its proper spread, but given the range and variety of plants at our disposal today MULTIPLE PLANTING could be uncommonly effective. The technique was proposed by other garden writers at the turn of the last century, but whether they were copying Chambers or whether Chambers merely copied and publicized a far wider practice we will probably never know. Multiple Planting, however, seems to have vanished with the passage of time. Perhaps it is time to experiment again.

It is interesting that Robinson never quite resolved the dilemma that most gardeners experience sooner or later: the conflicting claims of MIXED PLANTING and MONOCULTURE. On the one hand there is excessive variety, which if not carefully controlled can quickly turn into what might be called 'fruit salad' gardening – fussy, inconsequential and lacking distinction – and on the other the appeal of simplicity, of planting single species, related species, or variations on the same shape, colour or texture.

Robinson was one of the first to recommend broad sweeps of naturalized bulbs in true landscape style and the establishment of sizeable colonies of amenable herbaceous perennials in his woods, so they could become 'native children to the soil', as he put it. In complete antithesis of this concept, he also championed the soft jumble of cottage garden planting.

There is an impressionistic feel about monoculture – the broad sweep of a single variety, the perpetuation of one colour and subtle variations on some particular theme or texture on the grand scale. Even on a small scale such repetition can create a feeling of calm and repose and give the sense of a balanced composition at ease within itself.

Some of our gardening ancestors quite deliberately sought this sense of calm which is created by simple colour schemes. Islamic gardens had a small and controlled range of plants, principally of a cool green. The Renaissance Italian garden-architects almost exclusively used the Trinity of evergreenery, stone and water, generally a medley of greens and greys, as a basis for their designs. This gave, and still gives, these gardens a supreme elegance and distinction. In Le Nôtre's creations of the seventeenth century there was little respite from paving, stonework, allée or hedging except in the bosquets and parterres. On such a scale scatterings of flowers would have looked incongruous and rather ridiculous, although wide use was made of potted plants.

A great restlessness pervades many modern gardens today, particularly town gardens. Some time ago Russell Page, the distinguished garden designer, declared, 'The smaller the garden the more simple the theme'.[16] Golden words, but often ignored. We seem to have fallen prey to 'checklist' gardening, to filling small plots with a little bit of everything for 'rather have but two or three things somewhat large, than a dozen small ones which are no more than very trifles'.[17] Now each town garden has its obligatory puddle, architectural feature, varied paving and crooked line of sight, which, unless handled with skill, can leave the onlooker with a crick in the neck. Checklist gardening is also a passport to sameness, and there is indeed a sameness about many of our gardens today. But there is nothing new in this. In 1730 a garden writer complained bitterly of the 'general undertaker, who, regardless of the peculiar beauties of each situation, introduces the same objects at the same distance in all.'[18]

7 THE MAGIC OF WATER

A glimpse of water, even a swimming pool, through a veil of undergrowth arouses the interest and excites exploration as nothing else can do in the garden.

The third member of the Garden Trinity, water, is looked on by some as the greatest gift man or nature can bestow on a garden. Indeed the late nineteenth-century garden writer Thomas Mawson went so far as to say 'It may be questioned whether a garden is complete without water; if only a small round pond, reflecting and blending in thousands of beautiful ways, the hues of flowers, foliage and sky, at the bidding of every passing breeze, or but a swamp pool, hidden away in a cool froggy fastness fringed with luxuriant masses of bulrush, iris and sedge . . . '[1] We may not agree with all Mawson said but gardeners throughout the ages have known, welcomed and blessed water as an extra dimension in their gardens.

Moving water has an almost uncanny effect on the human spirit. Here is to be found the greatest attraction in garden or landscape and one never wearies of it. Watch it from afar, dabble or spash in it if they can, adult and child alike marvel at the Magic of Water.

As a view catcher in whatever guise, water is unrivalled, a tantalizing glint or glimpse of water moving or static instantly alerts the attention. Hence its use in a 'surprise' context, as a structural feature in its own right; water can also be a link and part of a gradually unfolding theme. As a vertical expression a fountain can perform a special role, while the gravitational fall of water in a cascade or emerging from a wall in dribble or spurt can provide yet another of its many moods.

Water can also be an important constituent of the bones of a garden either in static pools, ponds and swimming pools or in animated fountains, rills, streams or cascades. Visually, water can be a scintillating jewel or a mirror reflecting the sky. It is a canvas for changing patterns of light, provides reflection and colour unparalleled in the garden, and can contribute an audible dimension. Through the ages water has been used to play on the emotions and the senses. For in skilful hands, water can bewitch with a sense of peace, surprise or pleasure in a way unattainable in any other medium available to the garden creator.

In the earliest gardens water was present solely for the practical purpose of irrigation. Apart from the religious symbolism of the fountain of life at the centre of a four-square design, such siting also meant minimum carriage. But the practical was soon absorbed, although never completely, in the aesthetic and soon emerged elaborate and ingenious canals and waterworks. We can attribute much of our modern treatment of water to Islamic influence. The ritual washing of the feet was especially important so many of their water features were at ground level, hence the rill and the low burbling fountain which are characteristic of Islamic gardens.

Rarely then was the treatment anything but formal, usually relying on a rectilinear design based on a grid of canals which both sub-divided and yet united. In these lands shade, which also prevented excessive evaporation, was jealously preserved. The central feature of the Mughal Indian style was the pavilion surrounded by water and from which flowed the inevitable four canals of the River of Life, but within that grand design were a host of brilliantly imaginative embellishments, few of which are copied today. The formal design was common to an immense swathe of territory, from Mughal India to Southern Spain, embracing Byzantium and North Africa on the way. It was the style brought back to northern Europe by returning Crusaders.

A parallel historical thread can be traced from Persia via Ancient Greece to Ancient Rome. When the two strands came together on the steep hillsides of Tuscany and Umbria a special dynamism unlike any other in garden design was created. It is a dynamism which, after centuries of consolidation, is now beginning to break the bounds of convention. One can confidently predict a more exciting and inspirational use of water in all forms of garden and landscape design.

On the flatter lands of northern France use of running water in the Italian style was as alien as it was impracticable. Here water was incorporated on a vast scale which, despite sacrificing the sense of intimacy, became integral to the overall design. Indeed Versailles would be an empty shell without fountains and broad sweeps of water. These provided the essential movement, through changing cloudscapes and ripples on the *miroirs d'eau*, in what was otherwise a monumental static composition. And when the fountains were still and the whole allowed to decay, the detractors had their day. Said one: 'The artificial waters which are too abundant on every side are getting green, thick and muddy; they emit an unhealthy, enervating dampness and a still worse stench. Their effect is incomparable, but it can only be enjoyed with caution, there is nothing left but to admire – and run away!'[2]

There are two ways of avoiding such stagnation: by creating a balanced population of water plants which keep the water aerated; or by keeping the water moving, either artificially by means of pumps or naturally, using changes in level.

The COLOUR OF WATER, or the colour water can be made to assume, depends on three factors: the actual colour of the fluid, clear or brown and peaty, chill blue or almost luminescently transparent; the bottom and walls of the channel, container or pool; and the reflection of what stands beside, supported by the colour of the background sky. The permutations are endless as many of our ancestors discovered. Some of the Persian canals and little channels were shallow and

Opposite 'Express one main theme and how careful you will be to see that all your subsidiary planting and all detail shall contribute to your main idea and not distract from it.' (Percy Cane.) A succession of broad canals and limpid pools are integral to the garden design in the Alhambra, Granada, Spain. Water, as stone and greenery, was an essential ingredient in such Islamic gardens, but such repetition unless handled with distinction can lead to a certain sameness.

lined with coloured tiles, often blue so the blue of the sky was brought more profoundly to earth. Sometimes the canals, or in Mughal India, the tanks, were lined with black to give an impression of great depth and an air of sombre, sinister mystery. In Rome the little canals which ran in front of the xystus (covered portico) or peristyle (courtyard) were often lined with blue marble or painted cement. Use was also made of coloured waters to add extra interest although as far as can be determined there was no reversion to the Persian habit of letting the channels flow with wine or honey. What that did to reflection must remain a mystery!

In addition, water can assume a variety of brilliant colours when split into minute droplets. Light refractive properties of water vary enormously according to whether it is driven or free fall. Hence background colour, either solid, from a light source or from underwater mirrors, provides another fruitful line for experimentation.

There can be no finer commentary on the audibility of water than Sir George Sitwell's description of the fabulous water conceits at the Villa d'Este in Italy: 'And still one may listen to the magic of the wizard's music, for the muffled thunder of the great cascade dominates the whole garden, and above it, blended like the rolling of the spheres into the deep melodious thrill, are the varying notes of murmuring, mourning, whispering, rioting, rejoicing water.'[3] He does not mention, however, the sounds of water-powered automata which imitated birdsong and so delighted travellers in Italy and elsewhere in Europe in the seventeenth and eighteenth centuries.

WATER SOUNDS are an extra dimension seldom exploited in garden design today and looked on as a welcome bonus, rather than a pivot around which to plan the garden. The sound of water has always had the ability to stir anticipation, excite the imagination and encourage exploration. The Chinese and Japanese correctly deduced that nothing excites the curiosity like the sound of running water and exploited it to the full in their scenes of enchantment.

This realization was particularly appropriate to their concept of gardening. The 'stroll' garden brought to such perfection in the Far East relies on being able to excite the spectator to explore further and they admirably employed all the devices at the hands of the

Left Abstract design (in algae!) on the surface of a broad canal in the reconstructed garden in the Dutch style at the National Trust property, Westbury, Gloucestershire.

Opposite A place to dream. A small light-reflecting stream at Fontein Daniel, France. The impression of sylvan peace is enhanced by the restrained planting.

Garnish Island off the west coast of Ireland. A formal pool in a magnificent setting.

garden creator to achieve this effect – the disappearing path, the tantalizing glimpse of some hidden attraction and . . . the bewitching sound of water.

Here, 'The sound of the cascade, the shrubs half-concealing the ragged view'[4] draws like a magnet. There are few who can resist exploring a stream, tracing its course, enjoying its music, its planting and its joyful movement.

Evaporation from a body of water means that the temperature in its vicinity is substantially lower. Evaporation from falling water is faster, hence the temperature is lower still. The attraction of a cooler area in a hot climate is obvious, when to this is added the magic of a pool slumbering the sunlight, the glories of reflection, the play of light and shadow on surface or bottom, and the cadence of tumbling water all combine to create a paradise within a paradise, a subtle marriage of refreshment and repose.

The uses of water are manifold and as an instrument to create mood it is unrivalled, to the garden designer it is a weapon without peer in his armoury. It is a weapon that can and often is sorely and grotesquely misused. So what is the best way to capture and successfully capture this precious element?

Enthusiasm for incorporating WATER FEATURES in garden design is infectious. Pools and ponds, in many cases more like bathtubs, bidets or, as one garden writer said in 1709, 'Basins like Bowl-dishes'[5] abound. Some of these do capture the true spirit and magic of water but many seem to have been thrown down without regard to any of Nature's rules, let alone those of taste or style. Consequently, mysterious streams and puddles arise from bland lawns or some exiguous and equally improbable outcrop of rocks.

Like any deliberately placed feature, static water must have its proper setting and proper siting. The end result can be magical, or it can be disastrous. Constraint was once imposed by the availability of a natural water supply, but today modern electric pumps

Reflection, in a Japanese-style garden at Brooklyn Botanical Garden, New York. As in so much of garden design, reticence is more effective than the reverse. Bold grouping and telling shapes have a far greater impact than more fussy, inconsequential planting.

have facilitated the creation of water features almost anywhere. With freedom comes responsibility. The creative gardener should be disciplined when he comes to choose the site and setting for the new pond.

SITING should be considered as carefully for mood as for visual impression. What do we want from our water feature? Should it be static or moving, formal or informal? Should it be audible, perhaps a hidden source of sound which invites the visitor to explore? Or should it be a tranquil mirror? Does the lie of the land allow for a small stream and a chain of small ponds linked by miniature waterfalls? The practical aspects of leaf fall and the danger of creating a mosquito preserve must also be borne in mind. Most important of all, if small children are about, the water should be no deeper than toe-depth.

STILL WATER sited near the house ideally calls for a strict geometric plan to complement the four-square architecture of the building, particularly if of modern design, rather than a free-flowing natural one which is difficult to incorporate into any but the largest of gardens. However, an expanse of still water can easily dominate the garden. It will become the focus of attention and so must be used with discretion and restraint and as part of the overall concept. There is little margin for error in the siting and setting of water features. While it is easy to dig up and replant a flower-bed or border, most shrubs and even full-sized trees, the effort, not to say expense of re-siting or re-sealing a water feature is definitely to be avoided.

The simplest way to arrive at an acceptable solution is by staking out a sheet of black polythene. Not only will this show the precise expanse of ground to be taken up, but if pulled taut will also provide a reflecting surface not unlike water itself. At this point it would be folly to rush the construction. This expanse of water is going to dominate and dictate; it is going to create a more powerful feature than almost anything else in the garden. So before going ahead it is essential to consider it from all angles and if possible in all seasons.

Above A fine modern example
of the garden trinity.

Right An ingenious way to
provide vertical emphasis.

Reflection. Siting a swimming pool can be one of the most taxing problems in garden design. Here the simple white palings reflected in the blue pool create a memorable picture. The firm edges and the firm design of the background fence act as a foil to the looser intermediate planting.

Refraction. Here in a Hertfordshire garden the pool is hidden by a bank of foliage and a broad mixed border. As the viewer is so close there is no reflection of the sky or background scene.

Siting a large or a small body of water to the best advantage in a garden largely hinges on OPTICS, a facet which most modern-day designers are inclined to overlook. The positioning of a pond to excite the eye is all important especially the level at which one approaches it, be that from above, or below, down through terraces or up steps. In the latter case using the water as a mirror to reflect either the sky, landscape or seascape beyond is particularly dramatic.

When one considers the optical use of water one thinks of reflection or refraction. Reflection is the initial effect that one experiences approaching water and in Sir George Sitwell's view 'Water reflections are actually more delightful than the view they repeat . . . for the gloss of the water-film is like a coat of old varnish that mellows a picture, like the twilight it gives breadth, connection and unity.'6

At first you see the sky or landscape beyond, but as you get nearer the view is from a more acute angle. Then refraction comes into play and it is possible to see into the depths as well as being able to enjoy a partial mirror effect from the surface. It is from this angle, and from this distance away, that the design and colour of the bottom of the pool, combined with any movement of the water, become important. Most people give their pools a murky cement finish or a black bottom for easy maintenance when, at little extra cost, they could make it much more exciting by using tiles or small marble chippings. Olive-green, black, or a mixture of colours enhance the movement of the surface.

The siting of MOVING WATER must be dictated by the contours and the natural layout of the garden. It is perfectly possible to create artificial streams, but unless there is natural fall to the ground it is difficult to make them appear anything but artificial. In most cases, therefore, such water features are adaptations of an existing watercourse, preferably one with a perpetual supply. By the judicious use of damming, diverting and channelling, the most insignificant supply can be transformed into a permanent delight.

Visually, FOUNTAINS exploit the interaction and play of light on water, hence they are best seen when sited between the viewer and a light source. With modern pumping equipment we can make water obey almost any commands, even flow uphill! When we consider the immense range of fountain effects used by our ancestors, from the water extravaganzas of Italy and France, the restrained use of bubbling fountains in the Islamic world, the exploitation of the waterfull and water symbolism in Japan (where they employed no less than ten named types of waterfalls in their gardens) our own efforts and inventiveness seem inconsequential.

Where conditions allow, fountains are powered by the force of gravity, but the trend today is towards recycling. Technically, fountains can reach considerable heights, but an overlarge fountain can look incongruous in the wrong setting. The height of the fountain must be no more than the distance to the nearest side, otherwise the wind will divert the flow and no doubt drench the immediate neighbourhood.

Above Heard but not seen, the noise of tumbling waters has drawn the visitor to the twin, but contrasting cascades in a Wiltshire garden.

Left, above and below Water shutes with clear Mughal Indian origins.

95

Arcing sprays and low bubbling fountains are typical of the Islamic use of water in the garden, as here at the Generaliffe, Granada, Spain. The effect is to create a private paradise of bewitching intensity where the water cools the air and uplifts the spirit.

This constraint imposes an excellent rule of proportion on fountain construction.

Though the use of ponds, streams, rills, cascades and fountains among our water features is flourishing we do not appear to be as ingenious as our ancestors. An observer of a garden near Madrid in the 1620s wrote, that water, '. . . appears under the feet of the enquiring visitors, it falls from artificial birds that are seated in the trees in a heavy rain which wets you through; and other streams jump out of the mouths of animals and statues and wet you to the skin in a moment, so that you can find no way of escape.'[7]

With today's mechanical sophistication we could easily develop and improve on many of the water devices that have been used in the past. We must be heartily thankful, however, that the soaking of unsuspecting guests, who must after a while have become distinctly wary of further invitations, has fallen out of favour.

Above Westercombe, Somerset.

Left Waterlilies.

A simple yet highly individualistic design in water spurts in a Surrey garden. The multicoloured alstromerias in the foreground complement the varied tints of the red-brick wall to create a thoroughly satisfying combination.

'Wetting sports', as they were commonly called, were frequent features in gardens across Europe but clearly refinements more suited to warmer climates. Though it must have given a certain edge to a garden stroll, it seems an unnecessary hazard to have to wonder about the degree of mischief in one's host, or as one traveller put it, 'if the gardener befriend you not, you cannot escape being severely wet'.[8] There is something profoundly discouraging about running the risk of pneumonia after a garden visit. The usual game was to have little underground spurts at knee level, but there was delicious scope for the true artist.

> Here a Chimera opens wide her Jaws,
> And from her gaping mouth a Torrent throws;
> In her wide throat the crowding waters rise
> And foaming issue forth with horrid noise.
> There from a Dragon whirling round in Haste,
> On the spectators gushing streams are cast;
> Then with his arms and watching of his game,
> A brazen Huntsman stands and takes his Aim,
> To kill the prey, but shoots a harmless Stream;
> A pleasing cheat, at which the wondring Rout,
> At once with Laughter and applauses shout. . .[9]

It was even more fun if unsuspecting servants were made to run the gauntlet!

But this was just one aspect of water tricks. Some of these devices were quite charming. Perhaps amusing toys to serious gardeners but they would hold children, and not only children, entranced for hours. 'Curiosities' they may be, but in neglecting them we neglect a rather special facet in the use of water in the garden.

8 THE OUTDOOR ROOM

*We protest entirely against the view that there is one art of the house
and another of the garden. . . They rest on the same principles and
aim at a common end.*[1]

The term 'outdoor room' is usually associated with some adjunct to a house – terrace, patio, conservatory, atrium or whatever. But the true significance of the outdoor room is somewhat different. For here we find what man has always sought from his garden, what is in fact the essence of gardening, part indeed of our very spirit and soul – the search for a place apart. This private paradise, this inner sanctuary, has been called many things: in Spain the glorieta; In Italy the *giardino secreto* – the secret garden. It can describe a special corner, a place of security or of seclusion and one of personal intimate privacy where can be found peace, repose and tranquillity away from the hurly-burly of everyday living.

Perhaps this is what we seek in our gardens, peace, tranquillity and seclusion, and it can be achieved in the smallest of gardens. Here, in a garden near Newbury, Berkshire, is a modern pavilion, a 'glorieta' or private paradise. The elegant design and simple planting scheme avoids irritating distractions and the siting ensures seclusion.

The pleasure pavilions that graced the Persian paradise were places of privacy. Here, so we are told, were couches threaded with silver and gold on which reclined black-eyed houris of virgin purity and exquisite sensibility . . . or, for different tastes, a similar number of *ghilman* or silken youths. There would seem to be a number of practical difficulties these days in recreating this version of the outdoor room and the whole leaves one with an impression of clutter and exhaustion, not unlike some gardens today. Nevertheless, besides the attractions of their occasional occupants, these pavilions were light and airy, open to a view of a garden paradise whose firm architectural frame was softened by plants and the extensive use of water. Moreover they provided the tranquillity that is the special property of intimate formality in garden design.

In the Roman garden, loggias, or open-sided extensions of the house, porticos or colonnaded porches were alligned to take advantage of the sun in winter and soothing breezes in summer. Here too the air was cooled and the spirit refreshed by pools, fountains and artificial streams. Not content with the virtual merger of house and garden, the Romans brought indoors the perspectives and space of the outside world through the imaginative use of *trompe l'oeil, topia* (wall reliefs) and frescoes.

Similar aspirations are discernable in the Islamic gardens of Southern Spain. In many respects these are a succession of roofless outdoor garden rooms joined by passages and corridors with linkage between levels provided by flights of stairs either internal or external. Each 'room' is a private world with its own special character, but so expert are the links and transitions between them that the visitor is drawn on, and on, and on. These are places of shade and repose, segregated from the harsh landscape below. Three elements prevail – water, shade and colour, the latter principally from tiles and pot plants, although the main planting and growing frame is from restrained greenery.

In climates colder than those of Persia, Italy or Spain the concept of the outdoor room is more difficult to realize. Outdoor living is a pleasure only seasonally enjoyed, usually in high summer. Temperate versions of the Persian pleasure pavilion are the arbour or 'shadowe house', the summerhouse (sometimes called the 'cheesecake house' by the Victorians), the gazebo,

A reconstructed cloister in New York. The axial, cruciform shape, with a central feature symbolizing the conjunction of God and man was typical of many gardens in castle, manor-house and monastery in the Middle Ages.

Opposite Gardens within a garden. The design of this garden in Stollenbosch, South Africa, shows Islamic influence where different levels, different plantings and different themes are blended with great effect.

the covered walk and other corners of privacy usually sited in the sunniest and most sheltered parts of the garden, often away from the house itself.

There is thus a clear distinction arising between outdoor rooms attached to the house or building, and which more appropriately might be called annexes, and those physically separate.

As one looks back over the history of gardening the theme of bringing house into garden, or the garden into the house, recurs again and again. It is easy to dismiss it, certainly in northern climates, as the manifestation of a wish to protect those plants which would perish if grown outdoors and to garden pleasurably in a congenial, albeit artificial climate – these were certainly the thoughts behind the Victorian conservatory.

But the habit in Ancient Greece and Rome of building peristyled courtyards or atria in the very heart of the house, and covered xysti or porticos opening on to the garden proper, cannot be so lightly explained. These were carefully studied attempts to draw the peace and repose of the gaden into the house. It is this concept rather than that of the Victorian conservatory which prevails today, as we continue to integrate ever closer house and garden.

The mingling of indoor space with the view and reality of outdoor living has become an important theme in modern architecture. On the one hand we must cater for the pace of modern life, on the other, the fact that this very pace will create more leisure time. Strangely, the garden seems to act as an antidote to both, for, as we are told, gardens are healthy places, offering 'divertisement after a sedetary repast, pleasant refreshments after gross dyet, and such innocent exercises the best digestive to weak stomachs.'[2]

New construction materials have presented us with opportunities to integrate house and garden as never before. Our terraces, stoeps, backyards, loggias, patios or piazzas (according to where one lives) have become both extensions of our living space and spaces for living.

A seventeenth-century garden was described as being: '. . . like rooms out of which you step into another, the part next your house a parterre or grass plot bordered with flowers'.[3] It is clear from this that gardening to the very windows, which for reasons of space most of us now do, is nothing new. Special emphasis has to be placed on the transitional area

Right Simple solutions are so often the best.

between house and garden. Not only must this intermediate slice of real estate, which so effectively anchors the house to its setting, be looked at from indoors outwards, but also from outdoors inwards.

The hard-surfaced terrace or 'patio' is generally considered to provide this transitional area. (Although 'patio' in this context is incorrect for the original Spanish patio was a fully enclosed courtyard; today it means any paved area adjoining the house.) Terraces provide the platform to balance the house and give

coherence to the overall design, but they also help to integrate the outdoors with indoors – a theme which the Romans passed to the garden-architects of the Italian Renaissance, who in turn gave it to the formal French gardens where the privacy and orderliness of the salon were drawn out into the garden to create a stage of water, stone and greenery.

In designing terraces or patios the intention is to try to achieve a degree of stylistic interlocking and integration, either by echoing and taking outdoors the style

and material of the building, or, equally effective, taking the style and material of the garden structure towards the house. From the inside, the terrace provides a frame and accent to the view beyond; from the outside the abrupt change from natural growth to hard linear architecture needs to be softened. In planting such transitional areas, where walls, roofs and general structure strongly dominate, bold rather than fussy treatments are called for to lessen the impact of so much stone, brick or concrete. This must harmonize

with both the scale and the overall design of the garden. More important, the bulk and stature of key plants must be in proportion to such principal architectural details as the height of the windows and doors. The aim is to avoid a restless and messy effect which no amount of skilful planting can hide.

In less settled times when it was still dangerous to venture beyond protecting boundary walls, many dwellings had inner courtyards, made attractive in summer and winter with patterned knot gardens.

A true patio – in the Alhambra, Granada, Spain. Dignified, quiet, with restrained almost negligible planting and cooled by a simple burbling fountain. Here indeed is a place apart, a place for contemplation which is undisturbed by the world outside.

Right A modern 'glorieta' – a private corner.

Below The bold plantings of hostas and other large-leaved subjects, in this garden in Greenwich, Connecticut, produce a special elegance for an area which, according to the seventeenth-century writer, Sir William Temple, ought to 'lie to the best parts of the house, so as to be like one of the rooms out of which you step into another.'

Left The terrace of the same Greenwich house becomes an annex to the house. We are contending here with the four-square architecture of the house versus the less geometric natural shape of growth in the garden. Unless the transitional planting in such a situation is carried out sensitively, as here, the whole will jar. A simple design employing architectural plants provides just the scheme the setting demands.

Here, as our gardening ancestors were only too well aware, the principal enemy is claustrophobia. The higher the walls the smaller the enclosed space will appear. In Italy, France and elsewhere in Europe *trompe l'oeil*, as now in many town gardens, was used to provide the illusion of greater length or width. Sometimes these 'eye cheaters' were painted on walls, sometimes on canvas which could be folded away in the autumn and brought out in the spring. A practice which brought out the sharp rebuke 'What is the vista or perspective? A few sticks, a daubed wall, a cheat'.[4]

There is a special feeling of tranquillity and intimate unity in enclosed gardens, but structural scale is crucial for the internal planting can enhance or destroy the overall effect. The outer boundaries can be manipulated using see-throughs or by giving the boundary wall special colour or texture; depth or an appearance of depth can be created using climbers or taller wall plants, but everything fails if the central planting scheme does not conform to the size and scale of the courtyard as a whole.

Moving away from the house and out into the garden, there is an exciting range of outdoor 'rooms' for the modern gardener to consider. In larger gardens these might take the form of overhead structures such as pergolas, arbours, gazebos and summerhouses.

The conservatory provides a fine backdrop to this terrace and an old-time tea party in Dublin, Ireland.

Left A superb rose bower in a Surrey garden. The detail of the composition is worthy of close study.

Opposite In this corner of a garden near Newbury, Berkshire, the walls preserve privacy and exclude the outside world, and the garden could be transported to almost any urban environment. In effect an outside 'room' is created and this calls for special treatment. If the walls are too high there is a feeling of claustrophobia, if too low the sense of seclusion is lost. And if the inside planting is too fussy, the dignity of the surrounding walls is squandered. There is a tendency to dabble, rather than, as here, to employ bold groupings.

'Flowered rooms', as they were often picturesquely called by the Victorians, are often no more than a seat in a shady corner of the garden and sited for a particularly favourable view and sometimes without cover. In smaller gardens each nook or niche becomes in effect a 'room' and each can have its own special character. But large or small these are special places calling for meticulous planning and design. Essentially they are static areas of rest and repose, in many cases view-catchers besides and from where the outward picture is as important as the inward.

These are intimate areas to sit and contemplate, places set apart. This implies some form of separation or division, physical or spiritual. There is a strong flavour here of the territorial ambition which is part of our very make-up, the private places we wish to make

for ourselves. However, the 'feel' of the outdoor room can be created in other ways. The overhanging branch of a tree can provide the privacy we seek, and some protection besides. A seat under a tree creates a little intimate sanctuary where one can be alone with ones thoughts. At night this effect of intimacy can be created by lanterns or the judicious use of floodlights. And all help towards the attainment of our own private paradise . . . a garden . . .

> Where a soul's at ease;
> Where everything that meets the eye,
> Flowers and grass and cloudless sky,
> Resemble forms that are or seem
> When sleepers wake and yet still dream.[5]

Above Not so much a wistaria house as a wistaria castle! The sheer size and the elegance of the design, quite apart from the stunning canopy, dominates this part of the garden at the University of North Carolina, to create a memorable picture.

Opposite A dream summerhouse, or what the Victorians sometimes referred to as a 'cheesecake' house, in a garden in Oyster Bay, Long Island. Swathed in wistaria, here indeed is a place of complete seclusion.

A little corner in a garden at
Fire Island, New York . . .

. . . where a soul's at ease;
Where everything that meets
  the eye,
Flowers and grass and cloudless
  sky,
Resemble forms that are or
  seem
When sleepers wake and yet
  still dream. (William Butler
  Yeats.)

POSTSCRIPT

The constituents of our gardens are unchanged. We still have our plots, large or small, sloping or flat, town or country; our garden 'bones', ornaments and features; our plants in a variety of forms, seasonal or all-seasonal. Yet, despite technological change and horticultural advances, we arrange them in roughly the same way, and have done so for the better part of a century.

Maybe this is the way we want our gardens to look and we have been fortunate to find a style which suits our chosen pace of life. Or have we become hidebound, trapped by our own conceptions of what a garden ought to be? If that is the case we could learn a good deal from our gardening ancestors.

We are inclined to forget that they travelled the same garden paths we travel; encountered, then avoided or conquered, the same pitfalls we meet ourselves. The route they took to find their gardening paradises, in their own time and in their own way, is much the same as the one we take today. Except that a far higher level of imagination then was called for to compensate for their much reduced plant palette.

So now perhaps the time has come to examine what we are trying to achieve in our gardens, analyze what we have succeeded in achieving and consider alternative, possibly more appropriate, ways of attaining the same ends. Nearly one thousand years ago an anonymous gardener wrote:

The gardener must not be slothful but full of zeal continuously, nor must he despise hardening his hands with toil ... When at last winter has passed and spring renewed the face of the earth, when the days grew longer and milder, when flowers and herbs were stirred by the west wind, when green leaves clothed the trees, then my little plot was overgrown with nettles. What was I to do? Deep down the roots were matted and linked and rivetted like basket-work or the wattled hurdles of the fold. I prepare to attack, armed with the 'tooth of Saturn', tear up the clods and rend them from the clinging network of nettle roots. ... I plant my seeds and kindly dew moistens them. Should drought prevail, I must water it, letting the drops fall through my fingers, for the impetus of a full stream from the water pot would disturb my seedlings. Part of my garden is hard and dry under the shadow of a roof; in another part a high brick wall robs it of air and sun. Even here something will at last succeed!

It seems that nothing much has really changed.

REFERENCES

Title Page – Alexander Pope, Prologue to Addison's *Cato*.

CHAPTER 1
[1] Sir William Chambers – *A Dissertation on Oriental Gardening* (1772)
[2] Amherst Papers, British Library
[3] Humphry Repton – *Fragments on the Theory and Practice of Landscape Gardening* (1803)
[4] Joseph Addison – *The Spectator* (1712)
[5] Batty Langley – *New Principles of Gardening* (1728)
[6] Horace Walpole (Earl of Orford) – *Essay on Modern Gardening* (1785)
[7] Richard Payne Knight – *The Landscape, a Didactic Poem* (1794)
[8] William Whitehead – *On the Late Improvement at Nuneham* (1788)
[9] Humphry Repton – *Fragments on the Theory and Practice of Landscape Gardening* (1803)
[10] Alexander Pope – 'Works' (1736)
[11] Richard Lassels – *Italian Voyage* (1670)
[12] William Mason – *The English Garden* (1772)
[13] Sir William Chambers – *A Dissertation on Oriental Gardening* (1772)
[14] anon (quoted LM Villiers-Stuart, *Spanish Gardens*) (1929)
[15] William Shakespeare
[16] Abraham Cowley (1650)

CHAPTER 2
[1] Richard Cavendish (1520)
[2] AE Hawkins – 'Poems' (1868)
[3] William Mason – *The English Garden* (1772)
[4] Sir George Sitwell – *An Essay on the Making of Gardens* (1909)
[5] Leon Battista Alberti – *Ten Books on Architecture* (trans. James Leoni) (1755)
[6] Sir Edwin Lutyens – *Houses and Gardens* (1913)
[7] Alexander Pope – 'Works' (1736)
[8] John Constable – 'Memoirs' (1845)
[9] John Constable – 'Memoirs' (1845)
[10] Sir William Temple – *On the Gardens of Epicurus* (1685)
[11] Erasmus – 'Collequies' (1677)
[12] Richard Payne Knight – *The Landscape, a Didactic Poem* (1794)
[13] William Lawson – *A New Orchard and Garden* (1618)

CHAPTER 3
[1] Richard Payne Knight – *The Landscape, a Didactic Poem* (1794)
[2] Sir Uvedale Price – *An Essay on the Picturesque as Compared with the Sublime and Beautiful* (1794)
[3] Sir Reginald Blomfield – *The Formal Garden in England* (1892)
[4] Sir George Sitwell – *An Essay on the Making of Gardens* (1909)
[5] Sir George Sitwell – *An Essay on the Making of Gardens* (1909)

CHAPTER 4
[1] Sir Uvedale Price – *An Essay on the Picturesque as Compared with the Sublime and Beautiful* (1794)
[2] AJ Dezallier D'Argenville – *La Theorie et la Pratique du Jardinage* (1709)

[3] Horace Walpole (Earl of Orford) – *Essay on Modern Gardening* (1775)

CHAPTER 5
[1] (quoted Peter Verney – *The Gardens of Scotland*) (1976)
[2] Alexander Pope – *The Guardian*, No 173
[3] Girolamo Firenzuola – (sixteenth-century manuscript)
[4] anon (quoted Elenor S Rohde, *The Story of the Garden*) (1932)
[5] Francis Bacon – *Of Gardens* (1625)
[6] William Lawson – *A New Orchard and Garden* (1618)

CHAPTER 6
[1] Eastern poem (quoted LM Villiers-Stuart, *Gardens of the Great Mughals*) (1913)
[2] Sir William Chambers – *A Dissertation on Oriental Gardening* (1772)
[3] Hippolyte A Tayne – *Les Philosophes Francaises* (1875)
[4] William Mason – *The English Garden* (1772)
[5] William Robinson – *The English Flower Garden* (1883)
[6] William Robinson – *Gravetye Manor* (1911)
[7] William Robinson – *Gravetye Manor* (1911)
[8] William Robinson – *Gravetye Manor* (1911)
[9] William Robinson – *Gravetye Manor* (1911)
[10] William Robinson – *Gravetye Manor* (1911)
[11] William Robinson – *Gravetye Manor* (1911)
[12] Gertrude Jekyll – *Colour in the Flower Garden* (1908)
[13] Gertrude Jekyll – *Colour in the Flower Garden* (1908)
[14] *The Garden* (1899)
[15] *The Garden* (1899)
[16] Russell Page – *The Education of a Gardener* (1962)
[17] AJ Dezallier D'Argenville – *La Theorie et la Pratique du Jardinage* (1709)
[18] anon (quoted Elenor S Rohde, *The Story of the Garden*) (1932)

CHAPTER 7
[1] Thomas Mawson – *The Art and Craft of Garden Making* (1900)
[2] Marquis de Saint-Simon – *Historical Memories* (trans. L Norton) (1967)
[3] Sir George Sitwell – *An Essay on the Making of Gardens* (1909)
[4] Richard Graves (1834)
[5] AJ Dezallier D'Argenville – *La Theorie et la Pratique du Jardinage* (1709)
[6] Sir George Sitwell – *An Essay on the Making of Gardens* (1909)
[7] Cosimo Lotti (1620)
[8] Richard Lassels – *Italian Voyage* (1670)
[9] R Rapin – *Luton Poems* (trans. James Gardiner) (1718)

CHAPTER 8
[1] Sir Reginald Blomfield – *The Formal Garden in England* (1892)
[2] anon (quoted Nan Fairbrother, *Men and Gardens*) (1956)
[3] Sir William Temple – *On the Gardens of Epicurus* (1685)
[4] Earl of Shaftesbury – 'Memoirs' (ed. 1859)
[5] William Butler Yeats
Postscript – anon (quoted Elenor S Rohde, *The Story of the Garden*), (1932)

SELECT BIBLIOGRAPHY

ADAMS, William Howard *The French Garden* (1979)

ALBERTI, Leon Battista *Ten Books on Architecture* (trs Leoni) (1955)

BALSTON, Michael *The Well-Furnished Garden* (1986)

BARDI, PM *The Tropical Gardens of Burle Marx* (1964)

BECKETT, Kenneth *Creative Garden Design* (1986)

BLOMFIELD, Sir Reginald (with THOMAS, Inigo F) *The Formal Garden in England* (1892)

BROOKES, John *The Room Outside* (1969)

—— *The Small Garden* (1977)

BROWN, Jane *Gardens of a Golden Afternoon* (1982)

—— *The English Garden in our Times* (1986)

CANE, Percy *The Earth is my Canvas* (1956)

CHAMBERS, Sir William *A Dissertation on Oriental Gardening* (1772)

CHURCH, Thomas D *Gardens are for People* (1955)

CLARK, Kenneth (Lord) *Landscape in Art* (1949)

CLIFFORD, Derek *A History of Garden Design* (1966)

COATS, Peter *The House and Garden Book of Garden Decoration* (1972)

CROWE, Dame Sylvia (et al) *Garden Design* (1981)

—— *The Gardens of Mughal India* (1970)

D'ARGENVILLE, AJ Dezallier *La Theorie et la Pratique du Jardinage* (1713)

ECKBO, G *Landscape for Living* (1950)

ELLIOTT, Brent *Victorian Gardens* (1986)

FAIRBROTHER, Nan *Men and Gardens* (1956)

GADOL, J *Leon Battista Alberti* (1969)

GOTHEIN, Marie-Louise *A History of Garden Art* (1928)

HADFIELD, Miles *Gardening in Britain* (1960)

HAZLEHURST, Franklin Hamilton *Gardens of Illusion, The Genius of André le Nôtre* (1980)

HOBHOUSE, Penelope *Gertrude Jekyll on Gardening* (1983)

—— *Colour in your Garden* (1984)

HUNT, John Dixon *Garden and Grove* (1985)

HUXLEY, Anthony *An Illustrated History of Gardening* (1978)

ITO, T and TAKIJI, I *The Japanese Garden, An Approach to Nature* (1972)

JACQUES, David *Georgian Gardens* (1983)

JEKYLL, Gertrude (and WEAVER, L) *Colour in the Flower Garden* (1908)

—— *Gardens for Small Country Houses* (1912)

JELLICOE, Sir Geoffrey (and JELLICOE, S (Lady)) *The Landscape of Man* (1987)

JOHNSON, Hugh *The Principles of Gardening* (1979)

KELLY, John *The All-Seasons Garden* (1987)

KESWICK, Maggie *The Chinese Garden* (1978)

KNIGHT, Richard Payne *The Landscape, a Didactic Poem* (1794)

LACEY, Geraldine *Creative Topiary* (1987)

LOUDON, John Claudius *Hints on the Formation of Gardens and Pleasure Grounds* (1812)

—— *The Encyclopedia of Gardening* (1822)

McHARG, I *Design with Nature* (1969)

MASSON, Georgina *Italian Gardens* (1959)

MAWSON, Thomas H *The Art and Craft of Garden Making* (1901)

NICHOLS, RS *Spanish and Portuguese Gardens* (1925)

—— *Italian Pleasure Gardens* (1929)

PAGE, Russell *The Education of a Gardener* (1983)

PRICE, Sir Uvedale *An Essay on the Picturesque as Compared with the Sublime and Beautiful* (1794)

REPTON, Humphry *Sketches and Hints on Landscape Gardening* (1795)

—— *Observations on the Theory and Practice of Landscape Gardening* (1803)

ROBINSON, William *The English Flower Garden* (1883)

—— *Gravetye Manor* (1911)

ROHDE, Elenor S *The Story of the Garden* (1932)

SHEPHEARD, P *Modern Gardens* (1953)

SHEPHERD, JC (With JELLICOE, GA) *Gardens and Design* (1928)

SITWELL, Sir George *An Essay on the Making of Gardens* (1909)

TEMPLE, Sir William *Upon the Gardens of Epicurus* (1680)

TRIGGS, H Inigo *The Art of Garden Design in Italy* (1906)

—— *Garden Craft in Europe* (1913)

TUNNARD, C *Gardens in the Modern Landscape* (1948)

VEREY, Rosemary *The Fragrant Garden* (1981)

—— *Classic Garden Design* (1984)

VILLIERS-STUART, LM *Gardens of the Great Mughals* (1913)

—— *Spanish Gardens* (1929)

WALPOLE, Horace (Earl of Orford) *On Modern Gardening* (1785)

INDEX

ACKNOWLEDGEMENTS

The authors would like to thank the following people for allowing their houses and gardens to be featured in this book:

Mr Annesley 42
Mr R Banks 27
Mrs Pamela Barlow 54, 102
The late Sir Cecil Beaton 74
Mrs Robert Beyer 72
Bristol University 97
Brooklyn Botanical Garden 91
Contessa Marajen Chinigo 50, 64
Mrs Sybil Connelly (by kind permission *House
   Beautiful* Magazine, NY 49
Mrs Dillon (by kind permission *House Beautiful*,

NY) 109
Mrs Elizabeth Farquhar 19, 25, 26, 52, 80
Mrs Ford 112
Mr A M J Galsworthy, Historic Houses 38
Mme Garcin 58
Inchbald School of Design, London 24, 70, 84, 94
Sir Geoffrey Jellicoe (Sutton Place) 36, 98, 111
Mr and Mrs Martin Lane Fox 20, 21, 41, 99, 110
Mr and Mrs Masterton 7, 23, 32, 34, 40, 46
McMillen Inc, New York 106, 107
Mr and Mrs Tom Moore 114

The National Trust 10, 75, 89
University of North Carolina 113
Mrs Rhoda Partridge 39
Mrs Martin Richards 81
Mrs Ellen Samuels 101
The Earl of Shelburne 12, 95
Mrs Betty Sherrill 93
Tissue de Mayenn et Cie 88
Treasures of Tenbury 37, 55
Mrs Rosemary Verey 17, 51, 60, 67
Mrs Avary Wilson 31

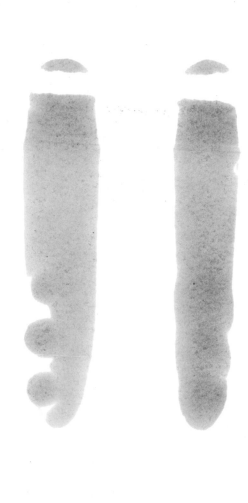